McCordsville Elementary
Media Center

WHAT HAPPENED ON
PLANET KID

JANE LESLIE CONLY

HarperTrophy®
An Imprint of HarperCollinsPublishers

Harper Trophy® is a registered trademark of HarperCollins Publishers Inc.

What Happened on Planet Kid
Copyright © 2000 by Jane Leslie Conly

For information address HarperCollins Children's Books,
a division of HarperCollins Publishers,
1350 Avenue of the Americas, New York, NY 10019.
Published in Canada by Fitzhenry & Whiteside Ltd.
A hardcover edition of this work was originally published by Henry Holt and Company, LLC.
It is reprinted here by arrangement with Henry Holt and Company, LLC.

Library of Congress Cataloging-in-Publication Data
Conly, Jane Leslie.
What happened on Planet Kid / Jane Leslie Conly. — 1st HarperTrophy ed.
   p.   cm.
Originally published: New York : H. Holt, 2000.
Summary: To help her deal with her separation from her family, worry about her mother's serious
operation, and suspicions about a new friend's abusive father, twelve-year-old Dawn creates an imagi-
nary world while spending the summer of 1958 with her great-aunt and uncle in rural North Carolina.
   ISBN 0-06-441076-5 (pbk.)
   1. Parent and child—Fiction. 2. Country life—Fiction. 3. Friendship—Fiction. 4. Family violence—
Fiction.] I. Title.
PZ7.C761846 Wf 2002   2001039855
[Fic]—dc21   CIP
                                                                                   AC

First Harper Trophy edition, 2002
❖
Visit us on the World Wide Web!
www.harperchildrens.com

For Chris, Sarah, and Kate

WHAT HAPPENED ON
PLANET KID

1

I'm sleeping in the barn tonight. The cows are breathing slow and steady, and Star, the old bay pony, snorts in the dark stall where she lies. The coonhound Red is resting so near my cot that I can drop my hand onto his sleek head. I hear mice scuttling across the floor near the feed bins, but Uncle Moody filled the cats' pans after milking, and now they're curled up tight as cinnamon rolls, bellies bulging, asleep in the warm, deep straw.

I didn't think they would let me sleep down here. When I was in the front room, supposed to be practicing the piano, I overheard Aunt Van say, "What about the snakes?"

"What snakes?" Uncle Moody asked.

"The copperheads—the ones that live in the foundation. What if they crawl up in the cool of night, to catch mice?"

"I'll have Red stay with her." Uncle Moody's voice was gruff, as usual. "He won't let no snakes come close."

"Moody, it's not like she's our child. If something happened to her, especially now—"

"You worry too much, Van." I felt like I could see his narrow face with its calm brown eyes, staring into hers. "How many days—morning and evening—do we go down to the barn to milk in the dark? We never been bit."

"But why tonight?" Aunt Van said. "Of all times, why now?"

"'Cause it's a comfort. If everyone had a barn to rest in, there'd be less business for these shrink-doctors."

Aunt Van sighed, and I guessed even from the other room that she must have given in, because she said, "I hope you're right, Moody."

"I don't hear no piano," Uncle Moody said. I started playing loud. He went outside and had a smoke like he usually does when I'm practicing. Aunt Van says he's got a tin ear. When she turns up that new singer, Elvis Presley, on the kitchen radio, he shakes his head and goes out on the porch to sit with Red. If Charlotte's visiting, we'll sing along with Van and try to jitterbug. Charlotte's daddy is a deacon; he doesn't believe in dancing. But we don't tell. After supper Uncle Moody changes the station, and we sit on the glider on the front porch and listen to the Senators' game. That's the baseball team in Washington, D.C., where I come from. Back there, in our apartment, my dad is listening to them, too. This year they've got a good team—four home-run hitters and the best pitcher in the major leagues. He signed a ball just for me: *To Dawn, from Camilo Pascual.* It's sitting on a little stand on top of my bookcase, in my room at home.

I'm a pitcher, too. I've got a target on the side of the barn where I throw curves and sliders and change-ups every day. I'm good—so good I'm pretty sure I'll be the first girl pitcher in the majors. I made the mistake of telling that to Charlotte. She says it can't happen, but I know it will.

The Senators lost tonight, 6–3, to Cleveland. Afterward my dad called. I knew it was him, calling so late. Aunt Van was in her nightgown, her thick white arms sticking out of the puffed sleeves as soft as dough. "Come quick, Dawn," she called. "It's long distance."

"Daddy? How's Mom?"

His voice was easy, like tomorrow was just another day; but I knew he felt nervous, too. "She sends her love and says not to worry about the operation. She says, whatever happens, it's worth a try."

I took a deep breath. I asked about my brother Timmy and my sister Beth, who are staying in Connecticut for the summer.

"Aunt Margie says they've settled in real well."

"Did you listen to the game, Dad?"

"Yep." Though he's far away, I could picture Dad's brown eyes twinkling like they do when he's about to second-guess the Senators' manager, Cookie Lavagetto. "He should have pulled Ramos in the fifth. If he'd pulled him early, after the first two runs, we might have had a chance."

"I thought we should pinch-hit for Lemon. But Uncle Moody says when Wynn's got his stuff, nothing can stop him."

"He's good, all right." Daddy stopped. "Dawn, I'll call tomorrow, soon as the operation's over, hear?"

"Yes." I think my voice trembled.

"Try not to worry, sweetie."

"Okay."

"Love you," Daddy said. "Mom loves you, too."

-☼-

Uncle Moody helped me get settled. He put up the cot with the quilt and pillow on it and a flashlight underneath. Though the two cows sometimes graze at night, today he'd shut them in. Star gave a low whinny when she saw that I was staying, like she wanted company. And Red plunked himself down and got comfortable, like he was as used to shuttling between the doghouse and the barn as a rich man with two houses.

It's good here, filled with quiet breathing and rich smells: cow and horse and dog and cat and straw and hay and oats. From where I lie right now, I can look out the Dutch door and see the blue-black of the hills beyond the house. The stars there are the same stars my dad sees from the balcony of our apartment on Sixteenth Street. I wonder if my mom's hospital bed is by the window. Is she looking out right now? Is she thinking, once I can walk again, I'll hike into the countryside and paint the stars above the hills?

I shiver, thinking about her lying on cold steel, with the operating room spotlights shining down. I think of the scalpel, cutting into her flesh, first one leg, then the other. There will be blood, I think; and I bite my lip until I taste my own blood, salt and warm; and after that I fall asleep.

2

Mom loved to laugh. I remember her standing in our living room in her red bathrobe, pretending the vacuum cleaner was a dragon with a long neck and a plastic head. Timmy would shriek with joy when she pushed it close, and his fat legs would pump backward, forward, like he was afraid, even though he knew it was a game. She'd stand there for an hour, doing that. I used to think it was a waste of time. I'd have my baseball cards all picked up, waiting for the rug to get cleaned so I could lay them out and study them again. "You're so serious, Dawn," Mom would tease. "Don't you ever just feel like dancing?"

She got sick the year Timmy turned six, just before Beth was born. At first they thought it was something to do with the pregnancy, the way her joints swelled up. Afterward, sometimes, she could hardly lean over and pick up the baby. In the mornings, when she got out of bed, she would stagger like a drunk on a TV show. Daddy would rub her knees and ankles until she made him stop. "It doesn't help," she said. "With this disease, nothing seems to help."

The disease was rheumatoid arthritis. Anybody could get it—even little kids—and if they did, depending on how bad it was, they could lose their ability to walk, to use their hands and arms, even to move at all. They'd be like frozen people, stuck in whatever posture their joints froze up in. There were lots of treatments, and some of them worked on some people, but nothing seemed to help my mom.

What made it harder was: she was a painter. Before I was born she'd taught art near the Smithsonian, and her paintings were exhibited at galleries and museums. I remember sitting in her studio, playing with blocks while she painted; and later, getting dressed in a red wool coat and leggings to go with her to an opening. Even though I was little, I could tell she was important from the way people asked her questions, and waited so carefully for her answers. "What you've captured here is the ineffable," a white-haired man whispered. Later I studied that painting, hanging on the front wall of the gallery, but all I saw were trees and snow and sky. Where was the *ineffable*? What was it? I searched for the outline of a small animal, maybe some magic creature like a unicorn, but I couldn't find any. Finally I asked her where it was. Mom burst out laughing, but then she saw she'd hurt my feelings. "Oh, Dawn, it's just a word . . . a way of describing how things look or feel. . . ." She put her arms around me, and I smelled her perfume warm on her neck, under her dark curly hair.

Compared to Mom, Dad's a regular person. He wears glasses and has straight brown hair, like mine, and he pays the bills and keeps the appointment schedule for Beth and Timmy and me, so that we get picked up and dropped off at school and the baby-sitter's when we're supposed to. When she gets excited, Mom stays up all night painting; but Dad's slow and steady, like the tortoise in the fable. He helps Mom figure out her business, too, because his work is raising money for galleries. He says he's okay being the right-hand man to fame and fortune. Not that we're rich—we aren't. But we get tickets to Griffith Stadium and the ice rink and the puppet shows at the Smithsonian. The balcony of our fourteenth-floor apartment overlooks the downtown lights. My school is three blocks north, and there're all kinds of kids there: white and Oriental and Negro, some who speak English but others who yak away in Spanish or Chinese. We think our neighborhood in Washington is better than the best pizza you ever ate, 'cause it's like a slice of the whole wide world.

But the farm is home, too. I stay here part of every summer, and we visit at Thanksgiving and Easter and Christmas. Van's really my mom's aunt, her mother's younger sister; but Grandma and Grandpa died in a car accident when Mom was little, so Van and Moody raised her. They're like grandparents for Timmy, Beth, and me. But Timmy's a city kid; on the drive home, he can't wait until the gray shafts of the buildings of downtown Washington appear from the ramp of the highway. Beth's different; she's never cared where she was. She'd wave her arms and gurgle in her plastic baby seat, happy as long as Mom or Dad was near.

That changed as Mom got sicker. At first she kept going to her studio to paint. She took Beth in the stroller, using the handlebar to balance the unevenness of her steps. When she got home she'd fall into bed. I had to give Beth her bottle, and sometimes change her, too, 'cause Mom would be asleep as soon as she lay down. After kindergarten Timmy stayed with Mrs. Glover, who lives downstairs. Later Dad had to hire someone to come to the apartment, 'cause there were times when Mom couldn't get out of bed. She had to use a wheelchair instead of walking. On bad days she was so tired and sick, she didn't even smile or talk. Sometimes it felt like she just wished us kids would disappear.

Later Dr. Bryant told her about the operations going on in Baltimore. They're experimental, so you have to apply to be considered, and only certain people are chosen. The surgeons remove some of the sick person's joints and put in new ones made of metal and plastic. If the operation works, and you spend enough time practicing, you'll be able to walk or write or pick things up—maybe not as well as before, but pretty well. On the other hand, the operations *don't* always work. Some patients get sick and have to have the fake joints taken out. Then the real ones have been thrown away, so the doctors have to bind the ends of the bones together, and they're fixed stiffly in place, like the arms and legs of toy soldiers.

I didn't think she should do it. After all, she hadn't been sick so long, if you looked at the calendar—fifteen months. Everyone said patients with rheumatoid arthritis sometimes got better on their own, for reasons no one knew. But the doctor said her case was very bad. The joints in her legs were already so messed up they couldn't heal. She was young, so if the operation worked there was a whole lot to be gained. I think that's why she decided to try.

We had to wait then, to see if she'd be chosen; but she was, near Easter, and they said it would take the whole summer to recover, even if everything went well. That's why I'm here. Timmy and Beth are with Aunt Margie, because she has twin toddlers, and a full-time baby-sitter. At home they get on my nerves: Beth squalls and pulls at my jeans for food and toys, and Timmy can't live without a record on the phonograph. He makes up words to anything—even classical stuff like Mozart and Beethoven. I'd like to hear his voice right now. It's high and sweet, and when he's singing, his brown eyes look faraway.

Beth likes to hear him, too. She'll push and squirm until she worms her chubby body into the easy chair with me. Then she closes her eyes and nestles close, listening to the music. Her red-brown hair is thin and soft, and it still smells like babies.

Maybe if that soft hair was brushing against my cheek right now, I wouldn't feel so lonely.

3

"Dawn! Wake up!"

The barn door slams and Charlotte's here. Her blond hair is sticking out every which way, and there's a smear of jelly on her cheek, and she's wearing a dress that's too small for her, so the back's gaping open where the buttons won't reach. She drives me nuts, the way she always wears a dress no matter what.

"Wake up, Dawn!" she repeats. "There's a possum playing dead in the straw heap. Let's drag him out and put him in a box."

"What time is it?"

"I don't know—who cares? Sonny woke me up banging a stick under the window. I went out to beat him up, and he showed me that old possum."

Sonny's Charlotte's little brother. She's got three older brothers, too—all rotten, according to her.

"Dawn," she says, "I saw a footprint in the barn-yard, and it isn't ours."

"How can you tell?"

"I'm telling you, it's not!" She pulls at the quilt. "If you don't get moving, that possum will be gone."

But by the time I put my clothes on, Charlotte's busy playing with Star. She kisses her on the nose, then starts to braid her mane. She claims Star's hers, 'cause Uncle Moody used to give her pony rides. Then the cows get shook up: Rose bangs her horns against the stanchion, and May, who's older and bigger, moans out loud. Just then the barn door opens, and Uncle Moody steps in carrying the milk pail. "They heard you coming," I tell him.

He smiles, pats May on the rump. "This here's my girlfriend, but don't tell Van."

He feeds them and takes the stool down from the wall. Soon the *blip blip* of milk on milk rouses the cats, and they're mewing, and Charlotte leaves Star and plays with Little Chief, the orange kitten. "You're the prettiest, prettiest, prettiest," she sings. "Wish my daddy would let me have a pretty cat like you."

"How's the deacon doing?" Uncle Moody asks. I know he doesn't like Mr. Williams 'cause he claims Uncle Moody's going to hell.

"He's okay," Charlotte says. "Got him a brand-new Smith and Wesson shotgun. Mama wanted the money for a freezer, but Daddy says canned stuff is better for you anyway."

"Heck of a lot more work for your ma," Moody says. "All that boiling and rinsing jars and lids. Freezing, all you got's them little boxes."

She shrugs. It's hard to tell what Charlotte thinks about her dad. Sometimes she says, real proud, "He's one of the Chosen." Other times I see her stick her tongue out behind his back. But if he catches her doing something wrong—even a little thing, like leaving a spoon when she clears the supper table—she scurries around like it's the end of the world.

Now she says, "Mr. Moody, can Dawn and me make a house in the loft?" When he turns to look at her, she opens her eyes real wide, like she doesn't know we aren't supposed to play up there.

Uncle Moody grunts. If I asked, he'd say no; but it's harder with Charlotte staring at him with those big blue eyes. He coughs and tugs at the brim of his cap. "Y'all can play up there a little while. Don't move nothing that's stacked up high, you hear me, Dawn? If you have to move something, move the loose bales."

"All right." We scramble up the ladder before he changes his mind.

Later, when we've dragged the bales around to form a double-high square and scattered loose straw on the floor, I ask her how she does it.

"What?" She looks at me all innocent, but there's a sparkle in her eye.

"Get them to give in to you."

"They don't always."

I wait.

"You can learn it if you watch TV. You got a TV back home, Dawn?"

I nod. We got it two years ago, for Christmas.

"See, we don't have it—Daddy thinks it's wicked—but I seen it over Fay Early's house. First you think of what you want. Then you pick a time when there's no trouble—nobody arguing, not bad weather or nothing, chores all done. You go up real close and you open your eyes like this"—she pops them wide—"and you look at the person like it's a favor, but not whining or begging, like Sonny does. With Sonny, whatever he asks for, you feel like belting him. You gotta make the person you're asking feel the opposite of that."

She looks at me. I nod as if I've got it.

"You wanna try it, later?"

"I don't know what to try for."

"How about fishing?"

Charlotte loves to fish, and I do, too; but we aren't supposed to go without a grown-up.

"Okay."

"Want to practice?"

"No, I think I got the idea."

I yawn. Bright light is starting to edge through the cracks in the barn wall, and pigeons are cooing in the rafters. There's something about their sound, sad and gentle, that makes me think of Mom. "I got to go up to the house now," I say abruptly.

"What's wrong?" Charlotte frowns. "You got to pee?"

"No." I don't want to tell her about the operation.

She doesn't believe me. "You can go under the bushes. Nobody will see you there."

"It isn't that!"

She sees I'm upset, and she's mad that I won't tell her why. "Go on, then, stupid. Take your stupid self up there. See if I care."

I hurry down the ladder and run to the house.

☀

But Aunt Van tells me Dad won't call til afternoon, 'cause the operation takes hours and hours. She cooks me a plate of fried eggs and sausage. Van thinks food makes you feel better, no matter what. She watches while I slurp it down.

"Didn't I see Charlotte here a little while ago?"

"She went back home."

"That's too bad. The feed store called and told Moody to come in late. He's got time to go fishing, if you dig some worms."

My jaw almost drops. I haven't even had the chance to do like Charlotte said, and here I am getting what I want, anyway.

"If you catch some, I'll make potato salad with mustard, the way you like it. That goes with fish."

"I'll tell Charlotte soon as I finish my practice."

Aunt Van nods. She knows I'm not talking about the piano; I always put that off til she tells me to, before supper. I try to throw pitches every morning, when it's cool. I break it up, warming up slow and then pitching my fast ball, my curve, my slider. I'm not allowed to start til the milking's done, 'cause Moody says the *whack, whack, whack* of the ball against the barn wall gets the cows stirred up, so they won't give milk.

But out the window I can see him coming up the lane with the bucket. He puts a screen and a cloth over the top, to keep dirt out. He'll set it on the porch to let the cream rise, and later Van will skim it off. When there's enough, she'll put it in the churn. She and I—and Charlotte, if she's here—will switch off turning the crank til there're pale, buttery lumps in the bottom of the jar.

"Dawn?" Aunt Van breaks through my daydream. "Are you done?" She turns from the sink, her hands still flecked with soap. I hand her my plate and run to the barn to practice.

☼

There's something about throwing a baseball that I love: the rocking motion, up and down; the way your head flies back and your leg goes out and your arm leads your body through the air. Then there's the *whap* of the ball against the wall or in the catcher's mitt; and you grab it as it comes back and crunch it in your glove and then the whole thing starts again: forward, back, leg, throw, *whap*. If that isn't comfort enough, the rhythm and the sound and how tired it makes you, there's other parts, too: the special fingerings or twists of the arm that make the ball go—sometimes—the way you want it to.

I talk to myself when I'm pitching. Sometimes I'll mutter, "Down and away," or "High and tight." Other times I'll hear the voice of Bob Wolff, the Senators' announcer, broadcasting my game: "Dawn Wesley's at her best today—great stuff on the fast ball and the curve's breaking just inside the plate. Here comes

Williams up to bat. He tugs his cap, stares out to the mound. She stretches, throws: 'Strike One!'"

Charlotte doesn't understand this. She thinks it's dumb, partly 'cause she doesn't know much about baseball, and partly 'cause, according to her, baseball's for boys. She thinks life's divided into categories: cooking and dress-ups and softball and horses and reading are *Girl*; knives and math and black sneakers and bikes and dogs are *Boy*. There's a few crossovers: eating, sleeping, watching TV. Once, I asked if she was happy being a girl. She looked at me like I was nuts. She said, "If a witch came along and turned me into a big old dirty man, I'd just go ahead and stab myself."

"How come?"

"'Cause they're mean."

"They aren't, either." I thought of Uncle Moody, and my dad.

But Charlotte shook her head at me. "You don't know, Dawn. You're like an innocent baby."

"Am not."

"Are, too. You don't know what's what, in this old world."

☼

She doesn't mind worms. When I'm starting on pitch number ninety, and my arm's feeling like a stretched-out rubber band, along she comes with a shovel. I guess she's been past the house and talked to Van. When she sees me throwing, she rolls her eyes.

"How many left?"

"Ten." I rear back and let one fly, showing off.

"Dawn, you're gonna bust that wall. Then you'll get a whipping."

"Will not." I bite my lip, concentrating; lean forward, back, let go. *Whap!*

"Mama says you're just ruining your arms. One's gonna be bigger than the other. What kind of boy will like you then?"

"Don't care," I say. To me, boys are a pain. . . . *Whap!*

"You better care. Dawn, I got bad news."

"What?"

"Mama says I got to take Sonny starting at ten o'clock. She got a ride into town with Mr. Moser, but there's only one seat in the truck, so Sonny can't go."

"SONNY? Fishing?" Now I wish Van hadn't told her. Sonny can't shut up. "He'll scare off every fish in the whole pond."

"I know." She sighs. "But if I don't take him, he'll do something awful, and I'll get in trouble. 'Member that time he tried to make a cake?"

"How could I forget?" There'd been two inches of flour over most of the kitchen floor when we came in from playing. Not only that, but Sonny'd cracked a half dozen eggs into the dog pan and stirred them up. We didn't notice, but Charlotte's brother Duke showed Mrs. Williams, and she started shouting how they needed those eggs for supper. I went home, so I didn't see the final outcome, and Charlotte wouldn't tell me, either. *Whap!*

"Dawn, I saw another one of those footprints. It was by the water trough."

"What footprints?"

"Girl, you already forgot. I told you about it when I first came in the barn."

I sigh. Sometimes Charlotte drives me nuts with her crazy ideas. "You ought to start digging," I tell her.

"I got my sandals on."

"Who's fault is that?" *Whap!*

She disappears, but a minute later I hear her yell, "I got a good one!"

Whap!

"I got another one, Dawn!"

Whap!

"I got a hoppy-toad!"

Whap! I throw three more and then I'm done.

4

Uncle Moody's taking us to Tucker's pond. That's about a mile up the road from the farm, behind a brake of cedar trees. We'd heard that someone caught a five-pound bass at Tucker's Tuesday evening, on a spinner. So we load Uncle Moody's rod and net and our bamboo poles and worms into the truck. Then Charlotte and I beg to ride in back. Soon as he says we can, Sonny falls on the ground, crying.

"What's wrong?" Uncle Moody asks.

"I wanna be with Sissy." Sonny's sputtering like a wet match. The knees of his jeans are torn out and his tee shirt has a purple streak down the front, like he's spilled a glass of grape juice there.

"Git in the back, then."

Charlotte and I groan. We make him sit, but Uncle Moody drives so slow Sonny probably wouldn't get hurt if he fell right on his head. We go out the driveway and turn left on the county road. Charlotte's family lives in a white tenant house to the right, where the road turns dirt. Near the boundary line are a couple of ramshackle places owned by Negroes, who used to hire on when there was extra work, like haying. The buildings are mostly empty now, 'cause the work disappeared when men like Uncle Moody closed their dairy farms and got new jobs. Everybody says you just can't make it farming anymore.

We pass a big brick house with a wide lawn: Walter Tucker's. He's got neatly painted barns, red with white trim; but his real operation's in the sheep fields and sheds by the river. We turn onto a dirt road, jouncing over ruts. Uncle Moody parks the truck. There's a path across an overgrown field to the pond. Sonny runs ahead, with Charlotte yelling to stay back from the edge or else he'll drown. We hear him whooping, and I wonder whose fishing he's messing up, but it turns out no one's here but us.

"Fix my worm." Sonny doesn't have a pole, only a little wooden frame with line on it for still fishing. He's already managed to get it tangled. Charlotte picks at it with her fingers, pulling the hook out and through, and gives Sonny a piece of worm. She sits him down at the shallow end and helps him throw his hook into the water. We go down the shore behind some bushes, hoping for a little peace and quiet, and throw our lines out by the water lilies. Usually fat sun-fish swim back and forth through the stems; if they're hungry, we'll get a good catch there.

"Dawn, you got a bite . . ." Charlotte points to my bobber. I thought the breeze was rippling the pond, but something's dragging my hook. When I tug, it lets go.

Then Charlotte gets a hard bite. She jerks the pole to set the hook, then pulls steady. We see a good-sized bluegill darting back and forth. When it gets close, she flips it onto the bank.

"Nice one!" We have a rope stringer with a loop in the bottom and a piece of wire on top. We unhook the fish, stick the wire through his gill, and feed it through the loop. Then we tie the rope to a willow bush at the pond's edge.

"You girls all right?" Uncle Moody's over on the dock.

"Yep."

Sonny calls, "I need more worm!" We groan. It's better not to have him close, but it means we have to run back and forth helping him. I go first. He's got his line snarled in a clump of marsh grass; in the mean-time minnows have cleaned off his hook. I take a stick, pull the whole mess in to shore, and give him a new worm.

"Sonny, don't drag the line right on top of a bush. Keep it out where the bottom's clear." He throws his hook in the water and sits down on the bank.

"When the bobber goes under, you pull, okay?"

"Okay."

I run back to Charlotte. She's already caught another fish. I grab my pole and throw the line in while she's putting her fish on the stringer.

"I'm going to get a big one now."

"You hope." She smiles.

But the bobber goes down, and sure as clockwork there's a nice fat sunfish dashing back and forth along the bank. I'm not as good at flipping them as Charlotte; you have to pull steady, then give just the right kind of snap. Mine's too hard, and the fish hits her in the leg: *splat.*

"Dawn, you made me stink like fish."

"Rub some water on it."

"No, I might get leeches. You know there's leeches in here, right?"

"Yuck."

Sonny screams, "Come help me! I'm tangled!"

This time Charlotte goes. She's cussing him under her breath. I guess she smacked him, too, 'cause I hear him bellow. Uncle Moody calls, "Everything okay?"

"Just fine." Charlotte's voice is pretty. A minute later she's back. While she was gone I caught another one. He swallowed the hook. I hate that. You have to pull out half their guts to get them off the line.

"If you'll string this, I'll take care of Sonny til we leave."

"You got a deal." Charlotte doesn't mind fish guts. She grabs my pole and starts at it. Just then we hear a splash and a scream from up the bank. I take off running. Uncle Moody hurries from the dock.

"I thought I told y'all to watch that boy."

"We were, only—"

Sonny's lying in the muck at the edge of the pond, bellowing like a sick cow.

"Give us your hands, boy."

He's hard to get a grip on, 'cause he's slimy. We tug and pull. Finally the mud bottom gives a belch and sets him free. We yank him to his feet.

"It drug me," he sobs. "My line drug me in." He hands the little wooden frame to Uncle Moody.

"You got this thing snagged good, Sonny."

Moody gets a funny look on his face, pulls again. "I believe you got something here," he says.

"What?" Sonny flies to the edge of the bank. I grab him just before he slides back in. A long dark shape twists under the surface of the water.

Uncle Moody says, "Get my net, Dawn."

I run to the dock and grab it, run back. He takes it with both hands and dips it in. Something splashes, drops back. Slowly Uncle Moody raises the net.

"Good Lord . . . ," I say out loud. Sonny screams. A fish with beady eyes and black whiskers stares through the holes in the rope basket.

"A mudcat . . . nice one, too. This here's ten pounds easy."

"Whoooeee!!!!" Sonny's whooping now. Charlotte runs to look. If she's jealous, she doesn't say so. Instead she says, "That's the ugliest fish I ever laid eyes on."

"Good eating, though." Uncle Moody tells us to pack up our stuff, 'cause we've had enough excitement for one day. Our stringer of bluegills looks like fish food for Sonny's catch. Moody throws the catfish in the back of the truck and gestures for us to get in, too.

"I'm scairt," Sonny says. "I'm not riding with him lest you kill him first."

"I can't—hide's too tough. It'll take a butcher knife or a hatchet to get through that."

I stare down at the fish. Its spiny fins are splayed out like it's waiting to stick somebody. "Maybe I'll ride up front, too."

"Chickens." But Charlotte doesn't want to be alone with the mudcat, either, 'cause she packs herself into the cab with us. We drive to her house. It looks pretty much like usual: there's a bunch of car chassis out front, and the porch is cluttered with straight-backed chairs and a couch that's losing its stuffing. Uncle Moody hangs the catfish from the clotheslines that crisscross the porch ceiling. It's so big its tail almost touches the floor. It's still breathing, and it stares at us with little beady eyes.

"You'll be dead soon," Sonny says; but he hides behind the fender of Mr. Williams' torn-up Buick. Later I hear from Charlotte that he stayed there til the fish was skinned and cleaned.

5

When I get home Dad still hasn't called. Aunt Van's got WYRT on the radio, playing Elvis, the Everly Brothers, Buddy Holly. She taps her feet as she slices the potatoes.

I go into the front room. The big black piano, which came from Moody's mother, seems to stare at me, and finally I sit down on the bench, thinking, maybe if I'm good, maybe if I practice without being told, things will go better for Mom. Mary and Jesus smile down at me from a picture above the couch. But the music sounds the same as usual: crash, bang, boom. I do a hymn, and when I sneak a quick glance, Mary seems to be making faces, as if she wishes I'd play something else. Just then the phone rings. Aunt Van beckons from the kitchen doorway.

It's Dad. "Dawn, the operation went great. The new joints are both in place."

"Is Mom awake?"

"Halfway. She's groggy, 'cause of the anesthesia. I'm going back to her as soon as I get off the phone."

Suddenly I want to see her myself.

"Can I come, Dad? Just for a little while?"

The phone is silent for a minute. "You know what we agreed on, Dawn; that you kids'll be on your own this summer, while I take care of Mom. I can't drive five hours down and get you and then bring you back."

I sigh. "Okay."

Now he sounds sorry. "I'd like to see you, too, honey. This is a hard time for everyone."

I don't answer. He asks, "Did you pitch today?"

"I did a hundred." I tell him everything: about sleeping in the barn and pitching and Sonny catching the mudcat. I feel better, and Dad sounds happier, too. He asks to speak with Van. I try not to think of Mom and her poor legs. But when Charlotte's mom sends up a slab of catfish on a plate, it looks so white and flabby that I almost puke.

"I don't think I can eat supper," I whisper. Aunt Van hurries into the pantry to get me a bottle of ginger ale. The minute she's gone, Charlotte grabs my arm.

"Dawn, meet me in the barnyard. It's important!"

"What's going on?"

She won't say; just shakes her head and runs out. I sip the ginger ale and tell Aunt Van I feel better, but she says I still look pale. She makes me sit another minute or two, then lets me go.

❖

Charlotte is bending over the mud by the gate, studying something. Her face is flushed. "Somebody's spying on us," she says.

"What?" I step back, glance around. The trees and buildings look the same as ever: peeling white barn, walnut trees, chicken coop, tractor shed.

"I know it's hard to believe, Dawn, but it's true. Remember those tracks I kept telling you about? Now there're even more!" She shows me a set of footprints. "They're too small to be ours."

I can see she's right. "What about Sonny?"

"He had on Rufe's old combat boots, remember? The soles are lugged."

Sure enough, these tracks are smooth.

"Could they belong to one of your other brothers? Jimbo, or Duke?"

She shakes her head firmly. "Sonny's got the smallest feet."

I bend down and trace them with one hand. They lead off toward the barn.

Charlotte gestures for me to follow her.

"See where he stood right here, behind this bush—he was watching you pitch. Then he snuck after you when you went up to the house." We see how the footprints fade, then re-emerge beside the kitchen window well. "I bet he was standing here listening," Charlotte says. "When he heard you coming out to go fishing, he took off through the garden."

Sure enough, the tracks head through the green beans, around the potatoes, and under the barbed-wire fence into the pasture that borders the county road. "Looks like they might go down by your place," I tell Charlotte.

"I'll look around the yard and see what I can find," she says. "I got to head home anyway. Mama wants me to help her cook that fish."

✧

My appetite's back by suppertime. We say grace, and Uncle Moody adds a special thanks for Mom coming through the operation. We just about clean up that catfish and potato salad. Then Aunt Van brings out a coconut cake she's made as a surprise. When we've each had a couple of pieces, Uncle Moody tells me to practice the piano. "Wash the fish slime off your hands, all right, Dawn?"

"I practiced already."

"Guess maybe I'll stay inside," he mutters, though I don't see what that's got to do with anything. We turn on the radio in the front room.

The ball game isn't on yet. Instead there's a news show from Richmond. In another state parents are complaining about kids saying the Lord's Prayer at school. The newscaster thinks they're dead wrong, and Aunt Van agrees. She says, "I don't know who these parents think put them on this earth in the first place."

Uncle Moody rolls his eyes. He and Aunt Van don't agree on religion. She's Methodist, but his faith doesn't have a name. Sometimes he says he goes to the church of the cow, the pony, and the pine tree. That makes Aunt Van mad.

Tonight, though, they don't argue. I think they're both happy that Mom's okay; though there's still work ahead for her. She'll have to learn to walk all over again. I think of Beth, toddling from sofa to chair to table, think of all the hands that reached to catch her as she swayed and fell and got back up again.

6

I sleep in the bedroom on the second floor. The air's thick as a blanket, and in the night I wake up drenched with sweat. But by dawn there's a whisper of breeze through the open window. I go down and pitch before the heat comes back. Uncle Moody's already milked, so I can throw hard as I like. *Whap, whap, whap*: my curve's catching the corner like I want it to.

Charlotte doesn't come, so I walk over to her house. She's on the side porch, helping her mom put laundry through the wringer. Charlotte stuffs it in, and her mom cranks. There're boys all over the place: Duke, Jimbo, Sonny; but not one of them lifts a finger to help. Mrs. Williams mops her forehead.

"How'd y'all like that catfish, Dawn? Wasn't it good?"

"Yes, ma'am." Charlotte's folks like to be called ma'am and sir, even by their own kids.

"I sure do appreciate Moody taking you kids fishing. We didn't have no meat for supper last night—would have been macaroni salad if Sonny hadn't caught that fish."

"Yes, ma'am."

"His daddy was so proud of him—just couldn't stop saying how proud he was."

I nod, but I'm looking at that pile of wash. They have five kids, so it's big. I wonder if Charlotte will have to work all day.

"Van said Evie's in the hospital. I sure do wish her well, Dawn. Bucky and I remembered her in our prayers last night."

"Yes, ma'am." Sonny's pulling on my leg.

"Dawn, let's make a fort. No, let's play cowboys. I'll be the cowboy and you be the Injun."

Mrs. Williams reaches over and pats his filthy hand. "So sweet," she mumbles. Charlotte rolls her eyes from behind the wringer.

I get an idea. "Aunt Van says the new potatoes are ready, if Charlotte can help me dig." I shift from foot to foot.

"Bless her heart," Mrs. Williams says. "I ought to get these big old boys to weed my garden. I didn't even put in potatoes this year, just didn't get to it, 'cause I had so much to do."

Jimbo's walking around with his hatchet through his belt. He's short and stocky, with a fat red face. Charlotte says he's a crybaby; and when he isn't crying, he's full of bull. "I can't weed now, Ma, 'cause I'm looking for snakes," he says. "I'm making sure there ain't no copperheads round here."

"That's good, Jimmy." Last year Sonny scared the family half to death by picking up a baby copperhead inside the well house. He didn't get bit, but after that they had to pray on their knees each night for half an hour, thanking God for saving Sonny's life. Then in May, Rufus fell in Walter Tucker's hog pen and got trampled so bad he had to go to the hospital; so they stopped praying about Sonny and started in on Rufe. They asked Mr. Tucker to pay the bill, but he said no. Charlotte says he's cheap as all get-out. Mr. Williams works for him, but he doesn't make much, just free rent and enough money to get by.

I'm about to give up and go home when Charlotte pinches her finger in the wringer. She yelps like a dog, then starts bawling. "It's bleeding, Mama, get the Band-Aids quick before my nail falls off. Oh, it hurts, it hurts!"

Mrs. Williams runs in the house, then she comes back with the Band-Aid box. She puts one around

Charlotte's finger. "Maybe I better get Duke to help me with this load. . . . Charlotte, I don't know why you can't keep your hands back from the roller. If I told you once, I told you a thousand times. . . ."

"Waaaah." Charlotte cries harder so her mom will know how much it hurts. Sonny sneaks up and grabs some Band-Aids for himself, but Mrs. Williams doesn't see.

"Duke, come over here and help me now. Charlotte's got to help Dawn dig potatoes."

Duke's the oldest and meanest of the boys. He doesn't bother to fuss, just gives Charlotte a look that says, *I'll get you back*. She scurries off like a scared rabbit, but as soon as we pass through the bushes and down the fence row, she busts out laughing.

"Dawn, I stuck my finger in that wringer on purpose. If there's one thing I hate, it's wringing out clothes."

I smile. "Aunt Van didn't say anything about potatoes, either. I made it up."

"Why, you, girl . . ." She grabs me by the shoulders and we hug. Then she says, "Let's see if we can find more footprints."

☼

They're there again: down near the barn, then up to the house, through the garden, and heading off toward

39

Charlotte's. Only this time we find them turned the other way, too; as if the spy saw us coming and hurried back, so he wouldn't be seen. "This is our chance," Charlotte says. We follow the tracks over to the corn-crib. It's a wooden one with open slats and a Dutch door. Right now it's only half full. Charlotte opens the top. "Could be snakes or rats in here," she says.

Silence.

"Snakebite kills you fast, and it's real painful." She's staring into the pile of corn. "Getting gnawed by rats ain't near as bad, 'less you think about their little pink eyes."

The pile stays still. Charlotte puts her hands on her hips. She's wearing a faded yellow dress with a short skirt and white plastic slippers. "I can't go in," she whispers. "I might lose a shoe."

"You think I'm going in, after what you said!" I glare at her, but she just smiles.

"I'm just trying to spook him," she whispers. I must be under her spell, 'cause I let her boost me up to the opening. My stomach balances on the edge of the door. Then I tip and fall straight down.

For a moment I lie there. The light through the slats stripes the dim walls and the corn itself. It lights up a spider dangling from a web up in the corner. I scramble onto my hands and knees. "There's a spider in here!"

"Is it a black widow?"

"I can't tell."

But the mention of the poisonous spider shakes me up. Then something warm touches my arm and closes on my hand.

"AAAAAAeeee!"

Charlotte peers through the slats: "Dawn?"

I don't answer, 'cause an arm is rising from the corn. In the dusty dark, a shoulder appears, then a head.

"Who are you?" I blurt out.

The head doesn't answer.

I take a deep breath. "What's your name?"

He's shaking.

"Dawn?" Charlotte calls.

"Come on," I say. "We're going outside."

❖

He's scared of the spider, too. He crawls on his belly over the corn, throws his hands on the doorjamb, and slithers up. I hear Charlotte draw breath on the other side. "Grab his leg," she calls. "Grab his leg, so he doesn't get away."

I'm too late—he's over the door like a lizard. But Charlotte's fast, too, and she's used to fighting boys because of her brothers. I hear him hit the ground, struggle, hear her gasp. By the time I crawl over the corncrib door, she's sitting on his back with his arms twisted behind him.

"I can't believe it," she mutters. She flips him like he's lighter than a dried-up leaf. I see a dark-skinned boy with close-cut hair. He's small and wiry, with a tough look in his eyes. "I don't know his name, but he's kin to Auntie Merle, at the colored camp. I heard he's staying with her for the summer, 'cause he's sickly. His daddy brought him down from Washington."

I stare at the boy. He stares right straight back.

"What should we do with him?" I ask.

"Tie him up and teach him a lesson."

"What kind of lesson?"

"Something so he'll remember not to spy on us."

"Okay." But I have to admit, I feel a little bit sorry for him, even then.

☼

I get some baling rope from the shed and Charlotte ties his hands behind his back. Then we half-walk, half-drag the boy into the woods. We tie him to the trunk of a sycamore tree, arms behind him. Charlotte puts her face up close to his.

"You been spying on us, right?"

The boy stares at her without moving. His stubborn expression reminds me of Timmy when he gets caught sneaking cookies, then claims his hand was in the jar by accident.

"We know you have, and now we're going to fix you good." Charlotte turns toward me. "Dawn, break off some green branches, the kind that bend. We're going to give this boy a whipping."

I just stand there. My parents don't spank me, even when I'm really bad.

"Can't we just tell him not to?"

She acts like the idea is stupid. "You can tell something a hundred times, but when it hurts, it sinks in deeper."

I wonder if that's true, and if it is, how Charlotte knows. But I don't want to hurt him, 'cause he's only eight or nine. "He was probably just playing," I say.

She faces me, eyes bright with anger. "Are you gonna get them switches, or do I have to do it myself?"

"No." Her bossiness is getting on my nerves.

"Well aren't you just Miss High-and-Mighty." She makes an ugly face. I make one back, but right then, the boy breaks free and takes off running. He's fast, too. Charlotte and I light out after him. He dodges through the trees, down a dry gulley, up the other side. We're panting by the time we get to the top. We look around—he's gone.

"Daag! That's what we get for fussing with each other." She shakes her head in disgust. "Now we'll never know why he was following us."

"We will, too." I'm surprised by the firmness of my voice. "He started it. Now *we'll* go back and spy on him."

But our spying mission is messed up by two dogs and a flock of geese, who start yapping and squawking soon as we wriggle under Auntie Merle's barbed-wire fence. She opens her beat-up door and peers out. She's an old woman with a thin, pointy face. The closer we get, the harder she squints. "What do you want?" she asks. Her voice is like a knife blade dragging on the side of a tin shed.

My mind goes blank. Finally I say the only thing I can think of: "I'm looking for the boy we saw a little while ago. Can he come out and play?"

Something—amusement, maybe?—flickers in her eyes. "No," she says. Her mouth is set.

"What's his name?" Charlotte asks.

Auntie Merle doesn't answer. After a minute she closes the door.

We sneak back in the evening, when the geese are shut inside their coop. The dogs must be inside, too, 'cause we approach with no to-do. A bright green Chevy's parked in the driveway.

"Where can we hide?"

The front room of the small, square house has windows on two sides, and both of them are open. There's a hydrangea bush to the left. We crawl behind it. A steady drone comes from inside the window. At first we think it's the radio. Then Charlotte pokes me.

"Dawn, I heard that commercial on Fay Early's TV!"

I stare doubtfully at the shabby tarpaper that coats the outside walls, but Charlotte's sure: "Auntie Merle has her a TV!"

We have to be certain. Charlotte raises her eyes to the bottom of the window. She stays put longer than I would have dared, then darts back down.

"She does—a big set with a wood frame! It's brand-new, 'cause the carton is still beside the couch! There's a man in there—he must have brought it. They're watching *Queen for a Day*, and the boy's sitting on his lap, eating saltines."

For a second I think of Timmy. He and I watch *Howdy Doody* in our pajamas Saturday mornings. Sometimes my dad makes us cinnamon toast.

"I got to look again," Charlotte says. But when she ducks back down, her face is red.

"Dawn, I heard them talking."

"What did they say?"

"Something. . . ." Even in the twilight I see her face getting darker. "Something about someone name of

Delbert. The man said he didn't want him chasing after no ignorant white-trash kids . . ."

But she doesn't get to finish. Right then someone opens the door, and a dog runs out. Charlotte and I crouch low behind the bush, but I guess it smells us, 'cause it starts yapping. We edge around the base of the house and take off. The mutt runs after us, barking and snapping, til we slither under the barbed-wire fence.

-☼-

Charlotte tells me the rest on her own front porch. It's not much, 'cause the second time she looked, the man was putting on his shoes like he was getting set to leave. That's when he said the thing about Delbert, and Auntie Merle started to argue, but the man interrupted, saying, "I think I'll let Billy out." The curious thing, Charlotte said, was that the boy looked to the window as if he knew that she was there.

7

The next day Aunt Van tells Charlotte and me to stay on our own property when we're playing. That makes us even crazier to spy on the boy, who we think is Delbert. Not only that, but both of us love TV. If we're nice, maybe Auntie Merle will ask us in to watch our favorite shows.

"We got extra eggs," I tell Van when I come back from the chicken coop. "Want me to take some down to Auntie Merle?"

She's suspicious. "Last time there were extra, you girls bugged me to make egg custard."

I lick my lips. The truth is Aunt Van's custard is the best.

"Anyway, Merle Dawson has a flock of Rhode Island Reds. They're better layers than these leghorns we got anyday."

"Maybe she needs some lettuce. Uncle Moody said the heads over by the fence are starting to bolt."

"She's got her own garden, Dawn."

Finally I come up with a good excuse. A truck leaves two telephone books by Uncle Moody's mailbox. I lug them to the front porch, check to make sure they're identical, then tell Aunt Van.

"You know how they got a lock on the gate over by Auntie Merle's? I guess the phone company couldn't get in to give her this, so they left it here."

Aunt Van's listening to Paul Anka. She thinks he's got a voice like silk. She nods, and I run get Charlotte.

❖

The bad part is, she's looking after Sonny. I can't believe we're stuck with him again. This time clumps of his hair are sticking up in greasy spikes. "He got into the Bag Balm," Charlotte says, pointing to the can of salve they put on the cow's udder. "Like to used the whole thing up."

"We can't take him looking like that."

She stares at me. "You want to rinse his hair out, Dawn?"

My shoulders slump. We head out, the three of us, up to the porch to get the phone book, then across the field.

Those darn dogs see us coming. The one that chased us last night starts yapping. Then he darts in like he's ready to bite. I yell, and the front door opens.

"I brought your phone book," I tell Auntie Merle. "See here?"

She squints at me like I'm a bug in the dirt. "I got mine," she says. She's about to shut the door. "Is Delbert here?" I ask quick.

"How'd you know his name?" Her voice is sharp. "Were you the ones under the window last night?"

"Oh, no!" "What window?" Charlotte and I are talking at the same time. Sonny's lying on the ground kissing one of her mangy dogs.

"Don't y'all bother us no more," she says; but before she can finish, the boy's there at her elbow. When he sees us, his eyes get big. Sonny looks up and grins.

"Come help me pat this dog," he says.

"Delbert, wait!" But he's out the door before she can grab his shirt and pull him back.

He can't take his eyes off Sonny's hair. He stands a couple feet away, then squats down so he can see it on the level. Finally, slowly, he puts a hand out and pokes at it.

"What you doing?" Sonny asks.

"W-w-w-what happened?" It's the first time we've heard him speak, and I see why. But Sonny's not sensitive like us.

"Why you talk like that?" he asks.

"Like w-w-w-what?" Delbert gets that stubborn look he had the other day.

"You know, all f-f-f-funny."

"You funny looking."

"Only put some stuff in my hair. Keeps it out of my eyes, see?" He tosses his head. The hair's like plaster.

"Lard?"

"It ain't lard, it's Bag Balm," Charlotte says.

"Lord God," Auntie Merle mutters, and she shuts the door.

☼

Charlotte says Jesus watches everything we do. She says He knows what we're thinking, too. He knows about my mom, and He'll decide if she'll get well. She tells me this as we're heading down to Auntie Merle's. Since we found out she has TV, we just can't leave her alone.

Only thing is, she doesn't like us. Most people will at least pretend, but she scowls when we come in the yard, and she doesn't trust us with Delbert, either. Yesterday she watched us out the window every second, like that boy was a gold-rimmed china plate.

Today he's playing in the dirt beside the house. He looks up and sees us coming, then scoots fast under the chicken house. I poke my head down. "Delbert, come out. We want to talk to you."

He won't budge. I hear him breathing hard.

"If you come out, we'll take you to pat Star. Star's like Roy Rogers' Trigger, only smaller—she's a pony."

He's quiet.

"Ponies are what short cowboys ride—cowboys like you."

Delbert wriggles closer. I can see him staring at me, wondering, maybe, how I guessed he wants to be a cowboy. He doesn't know I have a little brother, too.

"If we go to Lynville, I'll buy you a cowboy hat. They got 'em in the dime store there."

He's out now, on his hands and knees, looking up at me. But Auntie Merle's in the doorway.

"Why you want to mess with him?"

"We're not messing with him—he wants to pat Star." Charlotte's voice is sickly sweet.

The old lady looks from one to the other of us like a buzzard sizing up its prey. But Delbert tugs her skirt and her face softens. "Go, then, but be careful."

"Come on, Delbert." We crawl under the fence. He trots behind us, but when we get to Aunt Van's garden, he stops suddenly, his arms crossed over his skinny chest.

"N-n-n-not Delbert," he says.

"How come?"

"It's n-n-n-not my n-n-n-name!"

"Well, what is?"

"Roy."

"Like Roy Rogers?"

He nods, and we lead him to the barn.

Star's in her stall. I get a handful of oats from the feed bin. Her warm muzzle, with its prickly whiskers, tickles my hand. I show Roy how to feed her. Charlotte pulls the comb through Star's blond mane, sings to her. The pony stands still. She's too old to be ridden anymore, but she still likes being fussed over. I get Roy more oats. When Star's mouth touches his hand, he stands stiff and still, like a soldier at attention.

8

The next morning I finish pitching and head for Charlotte's. She's crouched in her mom's garden, picking something into a paper bag. Sonny's sitting at the end of the row.

"Charlotte got a whipping," he tells me sadly. She shakes her head, but I can see her eyes are red, like she's been crying.

"Can you come over?"

"Soon's I get done picking these limas." She's bent over, wearing a skimpy dress. I see red welts on the backs of her calves and thighs. She sees me looking and tucks her legs up close under her dress-skirt.

I help her pick. When we get to the end of the row her bag's halfway full. We go to the kitchen door to ask if she can leave. Mrs. Williams looks tired and sad—her brown hair hangs limp around her neck, and the skin on her hands is raw. She hefts the bag. Her voice is kind. "They got to be shelled, honey."

"Can't I do that later?" Charlotte's eyes aren't open wide this time.

"Just be sure you're home in time." Her mom doesn't look right at her, but she touches Charlotte's arm, just for a minute. We get out of there before she tells us to take Sonny, too.

☼

I try to cheer Charlotte up as we wind our way along the fencerow. "Want to listen to the radio? We could play Parcheesi, too."

"Nah, let's make a house."

"Where?"

She stops to think. "How 'bout in that patch of jimsonweed down near the brook? It's so thick, they'll never find us there."

We get a sickle and a machete from the toolshed. The jimsonweed rattles above our heads. We make a narrow path; then when we get near the middle of the patch we clear a circle ten feet wide. We stuff a couple burlap bags with straw to use as pillows, drag out some wooden crates, a mason jar filled with water, a couple of cracked cups, my copies of Nancy Drew, and a dirty book Charlotte snitched from under Jimbo's bed. It's got a scene where a cowboy kisses a woman and tries to touch her breast. When Charlotte and I read the words out loud, we crack up laughing.

Later we play house: I'm the father and Charlotte's the mother.

"I'm glad we ain't got no baby," she says. "I don't want no man touching me ever." She lies back on her burlap bags. The sky is a circle above the gray-green jimsonweed. "Look, Dr. Davis"—that's what she calls me, though we're supposed to be married—"you can see the moon."

Sure enough, it's rising watery white in the dark blue. For some reason I think of our apartment at home, how you can see the moon from the metal chairs out on the balcony. My mom and dad used to sit there sipping martinis on summer evenings. Sometimes they made Timmy and me fancy drinks, too, with ginger ale and slices of orange and a cherry on a toothpick. There are trees alongside our building: an oak, an elm, and a sycamore; but you have to walk three blocks to get to the park. I used to take Timmy and Beth there in the afternoons, when Mom was sick.

"How's your ma?" she asks, as if she read my mind. "Can she walk now?"

"No—that'll take all summer, 'cause she has to learn to walk again."

"What if she can't?"

I never thought of that, and I don't want to now. "She can," I say.

"Oh." Charlotte sits up, stares at me. "My ma knew her, back when your ma was little. They'd play together now and then. Ma said she always knew your ma wasn't going to marry anyone from here. Didn't guess she'd end up crippled, though."

"She's not!"

Charlotte doesn't look at me. "Guess I better shell those limas." She hides the burlap pillows, tucks the rest of our stuff underneath a plastic bag. Then she waves and heads across the fields toward home.

❖

Later I see Roy. We pat Star a while, then walk up to the house. Aunt Van's got her radio on in the kitchen, and I notice Roy tapping his feet, like Timmy does. "Do you like music?"

He nods.

"I can play the piano—want to hear?"

We go in the back door. The phone rings, and Van answers it. I slide onto the piano bench, pat the empty space beside me. Then I bang out "God Bless America," which I know by heart. Roy looks stunned. He touches the piano keys gently with one hand.

"Want me to show you how to do a scale?"

He nods. I do the C scale. I'm good on that one.

Then I notice his eyes: like a puppy begging for a biscuit. I put his thumb on middle C. He plays the scale quiet, but he gets it right. I can't believe my ears—it took me a couple of months to master that thing.

"Bet you can't do this." I play "Chopsticks." He's watching real close. The minute I'm done he puts his hands just where mine were and does the whole thing right!

"How 'bout this?" I know I've got him now. I play "Onward, Christian Soldiers," which has chords in the bass part. Sure enough, he can't do it; but he plays the melody with hardly a mistake. He does it different from me: softer, and like the notes are friends. Suddenly I figure it out. "You've had lessons, haven't you, Roy?"

He shakes his head.

"Do that again, Dawn," Aunt Van calls from the kitchen. "That sounded good."

9

Saturday, Charlotte's brother Rufus gets the kids together for a baseball game. I ask if Roy can come; he nods and says, "Why not?" It turns out three colored boys from a cabin near Miller's store are playing, too.

"How'd Rufe get up such a crowd?" I ask Charlotte. She shrugs. Rufe's the nicest of the Williams boys; he's fourteen, a tall redhead, with gangly arms and legs. He's always been weird, but the accident in the hog pen made him even stranger. He had convulsions, and while he was in the hospital being treated he fell in love with a nurse, Lois, who's forty-one years old. He keeps her picture in his pocket. When his daddy tried to tear it up, Rufe threw a fit, saying his seizures would come back. Mr. Williams backed off then. Charlotte said Lois and the doctors told her dad he couldn't beat Rufe ever again, 'cause he's delicate.

"How'd they know he had?" I ask.

"Saw his back. Guess they knew them scars didn't come from no hogs."

"Why'd he do that to him, anyway?"

"He tried to teach him right from wrong, 'cause Rufe's in dreamland. Daddy'd send him to milk, he'd come back with a handful of mushrooms or some empty Pepsi bottles. Didn't even remember what he was supposed to do." She shook her head slowly. "Could be he's simple; that's what Mama thinks. But I think he just don't care."

But he runs the baseball game, naming Jimbo and Duke as captains and letting them choose up sides. Duke picks mostly boys, leaving me, Charlotte, and Roy. Jimbo's mad, 'cause he figures we're three outs. But he lets me pitch, since he wants his good fielders at first base and in the outfield. I start with a strikeout on Wally Tucker. Then I get one against Dick Young, who Sonny says can hit. Dick stares at me after his third strike, his mouth turns down, and he spits on the ground. Duke's mad. He grabs the bat and steps up to the plate. "Just throw that sinker-ball on me."

I go back to the mound, which is nothing but an old rubber tire mostly buried in dirt. Duke waves the bat over his head. My first pitch is outside, and he holds back. Then I put a fast ball down the middle. He gets a piece of it and fouls it off. I break a curve on the inside. He steps back and muscles a line drive right at me, and I grab it just above my head. Duke cusses. One of the colored boys in our outfield laughs at him: "Got you, huh, Big Cookie?"

But during our ups we don't do much better. Charlotte strikes out fast, then Rufe pops a ball to first. Jimbo gets a hit, but Mickey Kettle, the boy who teased Duke, strikes out on a pitch way over his head. My next inning isn't quite as good, but I get a strike-out on Sonny before Sam Kettle hits a ball to center. The ball flies high and the center fielder yells, "I got it!" then he lets it fall. Sam scoots all the way to third. Duke is laughing: "Got you now." I give Wally Tucker a couple low balls, then throw a sidearm pitch, which he bites on. It's a dribbler right to first. Jimbo gets the out, but Sam crosses the plate. They're hooting about how good they are. "You're only one run up," Rufe says.

And I get the next two on strikes. Then we're up, and I face Duke. He's big, with dark hair and eyebrows, and he glares in at the plate. He throws one near my head and I back off, then I miss three straight. Jimbo hits one past third base, then Mickey knocks a grounder up the middle. It's a hard play, but a better fielding pitcher would have had it. Now Roy's up. He stares at Duke with that same stubborn look he had when we caught him by the corncrib. Duke pitches: "Strike One!" But I can see Roy's played before; his practice swings are level, and he bunts the next pitch down the third-base line. Peggy Young stands there looking at it, and both our runners score. "How 'bout that! I'm going to call you Little Willie Mays!" Mickey's jumping up and down on the sideline. Roy looks in from second, smiling.

Then we score three more, and the game breaks loose. Duke gets mad and quits. Peggy Young claims she got a bee sting. We redivide the teams and play for fun, pitching to each kid until they get a hit. Charlotte stands at the plate ten minutes before the bat touches the ball. By then we're rolling on the ground, laughing, and she makes it all the way around: "Home Run!" Rufe's picking dandelions in the outfield. Then Aunt Van calls she's made us lemonade, and we troop up on the porch. We drink it from a dipper. Van gives the colored boys a separate one.

10

Charlotte and I make a plan to trick the boys. We pick Roy up at home, but as soon as we slide under the fence, he stops and says, "N-n-n-not Roy!"

"Now what?" we ask.

"W-w-w-w-willie!"

We go down to the barn. There's an old bandana stashed there, but when he sees we want to blindfold him, Willie shakes his head. But Charlotte smiles and opens her eyes real wide til he says yes.

We lead him around a while, so he won't know where we're headed. Then we take him through the path to the clearing. I pull out one of the burlap pillows: "You can sit down now." We take off the bandana. He's looking all around.

"We're in a special place," Charlotte says. "You got to promise not to tell."

He sits there for a minute, looking. Finally he raises one hand.

"You're swearing not to tell, right, Willie?" Charlotte's voice is tough.

He nods.

"Okay." She turns. "You tell him, Dawn."

Of course, the big lie falls on me. I sigh, but the story we agreed on comes easy: "You may not believe this, Willie, but after we blindfolded you, we went through a gate between two trees. Once you go through it, you leave the regular world."

His eyes get big.

"I don't want you to feel upset, 'cause we can get back home as soon as we need to—if I snapped my fingers, I could have you back right now. But the truth is, we're on another planet."

He jumps up. For a minute I think he's going to run.

"Don't," Charlotte says. "It could be dangerous. We don't know everything that's here."

"But it's mostly good," I say hurriedly. "Because this planet is run by girls. There're no grown-ups here, and the only boys are nice ones who are specially invited—like you."

Charlotte nods. "Only thing is, we haven't finished exploring it. There could be wild animals we don't know about."

"We've ordered a bunch of khaki suits and helmets in our sizes, but they haven't come yet. We're going to get some pistols and machetes, too, and baseball bats."

"Baseball bats?" Charlotte frowns.

"Yeah, 'cause the teams up here are girl teams. They're all-powerful. They can beat the Yankees with one hand behind their backs."

Willie looks from one of us to the other. He's suspicious. "Wh-wh-what's it called?"

I think fast. "Planet Kid. You'll see things that remind you of home." I go on: "Trees and animals and sky. It's the people that are different."

"Did anybody else come?"

"Not yet, but one day I might bring Sonny, if he's good." Charlotte rolls her eyes at me, since we both know Sonny can never be good. "But you won't know about it, 'cause one of the rules is, you can't talk about Planet Kid on Earth. If you do, you'll drop dead."

That's too much for Willie. He starts crying. "Want me to take you back?" I ask. He nods, and I blindfold him and lead him out. When we get to the barnyard, I slip off the bandana. "You're home, see?"

He doesn't smile, but a shudder of relief runs down his back.

I take him with me while I practice the piano, slipping him in like I did before. Van's in the kitchen; she calls to me and I answer. Then I start off like last time: C scale. Soon's I'm done, Willie does it, too.

Next I do F, then G. He watches carefully, then repeats, only softer. He's getting everything right. I play "Yankee Doodle." He loves that. Soon as I finish, he picks out the melody. He plays it lively, like a dance tune. I'm starting to think he's a musical genius. Maybe somebody should know about this.

But not Aunt Van. She thinks it's all me, and she loves it. "Your mama's going to be so pleased," she calls from the other room. "She always said it was just a matter of time before you caught on."

I don't answer, but Willie grins, 'cause he's got something on me.

11

The next day, Mom calls. I can't stop smiling once I hear how good she sounds. She asks me what I'm up to.

"Nothing, really."

"How's Star?"

"She's good—we brush her every day."

"Are you doing your pitching?"

"Yeah, and I got to pitch in a game. I struck six kids out." I tell her all about it.

"Wonderful! How's the piano coming along?"

"Uhhh . . . there's a little boy from Washington, he's here for the summer, too. I'm teaching him to play."

"That's great. . . ." We talk and talk. She'll go to physical therapy tomorrow. She asks about Charlotte.

"She's fine. We made a special place out in the jimsonweeds."

"A fort?"

"Kind of . . ." We said we wouldn't talk about Planet Kid.

"That sounds like fun," Mom says.

※

Charlotte's mad I get to live in Washington. She's never been there, never been to any big city except Richmond, and she only went there 'cause Rufe was in the hospital. Sonny lies and says he's visited New York. We ask him what he saw.

"The Umpire State Building." His lower lip is sticking out. "It's the biggest darn building in the whole wide world."

"What else?"

He frowns. "I seen a lot of cars and trucks."

"Did you see farms?" Charlotte asks sweetly.

"Yeah, I seen farms. One farm had a dairy bull with a ring in its nose."

Charlotte and I burst out laughing. "Ain't no farms in New York City, stupid," she says.

But Sonny's stubborn as can be. He crosses his arms over his filthy tee shirt. They're covered with bruises from him falling down and being places he never should have been. "I seen that dairy bull," he repeats. "It was tied to the bottom of the Umpire State Building, and they had a *For Sale* sign right next to it."

"Sonny," Charlotte says, "you're a jackass liar."

"Am not." He glares. "How would you know, anyway? You ain't never been to New York."

"I'll get there, though. I don't plan to spend my whole life sweating in the damn pea patch."

His eyes turn deep, and his words sound more worried than threatening. "If Daddy hears you cuss, you'll get a whipping."

"Will not," she says; but something flickers across her face, like the shadow a flying bird makes on dark leaves. "Don't tell, all right, Sonny?"

"I won't tell," he says.

❖

Willie's got a new name: Glad. He won't tell us where it's from, but Rufe says he was sitting with him, watching Ted Mack's *Original Amateur Hour*, when a colored girl won the talent show by singing gospel. Rufe says her name was Gladys Knight. "After that he wouldn't let me call him Willie no more."

Rufe's hands are deep in his pockets, so his elbows poke out from his sides, and he's whistling. Charlotte grabs his arm. "Rufus Wade Williams, I can't believe you watched TV without me."

"You wasn't anyplace around." He smiles, and you can see a gap in his front teeth. He picks up a fishing pole from the pile of junk on their front porch.

"Where you going?" Charlotte demands.

"Me and Glad and Mickey Kettle is going fishing."

"You're not really going to call him that!" Charlotte stares at Rufe, but he doesn't even blink.

"Why not?"

"Glad's a girl's name."

He shrugs. Charlotte's about to argue, then she changes her mind. "Let me and Dawn come, too, okay?"

"You ain't watching Sonny, are you? I can't catch crap with Sonny." Rufe lowers his voice, just in case. I don't think he's as stupid as people say.

"He's in the house with Mama. Let's go now, before she sees us here and sends him out to play."

☼

I don't ask Aunt Van. We walk the mile through Walter Tucker's to the river. It's pretty back there: sycamores and willows overreach the water, and there're big flat rocks to sit on, too. You can hear the sheep bleating in the fields a quarter mile back. Rufe says this stretch of land was once an Indian camp; if you come in spring, after they plow, you'll find a handful of arrowheads. He tells us foods they used to eat: wild asparagus, groundnuts, chinquapins.

We throw our lines out. It's hot, and the fish are slow rising to the bait. "Laying on the bottom," Rufe says. He ties a rock-sinker to his line, catches a sun-fish. The rest of us scramble around the mossy bank, finding pebbles and tying them on.

But the fish won't bite. The boys decide to go swimming. Charlotte wants to, too, and so do I. I'm wearing shorts, but she's got a dress on. She holds it up and goes in up to her ankles, then her knees. She splashes water toward me: "Come on, Dawn."

I shake my head, 'cause I'm not allowed to swim without a grown-up; but I'm sweating like crazy. Charlotte says, "Give me your shorts, 'cause this dress is getting in my way."

"No, I'm coming in myself." I take my shoes off and wade in. The current swirls around my neck. But the sight of my fishing pole pulls me back, and I climb out, feeling cool and clean. The others are so noisy I end up moving down the bank. At the end of a stand of willows I catch a small-mouth bass on a grasshopper. I try to show them, but they're having too much fun to pay attention: their shoulders and chests gleam as they kick up and dive under, turning somersaults. Charlotte's taken off her dress so she can play, too. The white bottom of her underwear surfaces just a second as she tumbles forward. She comes up gasping and laughing.

Then we leave. The boys wring out their shirts and roll them up like towels. Glad stays right by Mickey.

Charlotte's got her dress on, but there're dark patches around her rump and front from her soaking-wet underwear. We cut across the fields. Men are out working the sheep, calling back and forth; Walter Tucker's there, too, in his fancy new pickup. We hear him yell: "You fool! I'll have to do the whole thing over!"

The other person's hidden. Then the truck speeds off, leaving him in front of us. Rufe mutters, "Charlotte, run!" There's a row of cedars to our left.

But she's frozen like a statue, like one of those children with arthritis, who can't move their arms and legs. Her daddy's staring. He comes across the field with such long strides it looks like he's on stilts. His blue eyes bore into us like the ray-gun beams on *Captain Midnight*. They pass over Charlotte, the damp patches on her dress.

He grabs her. "How come you're wet?"

"B-b-b-been swimming in the river."

"Naked?" He raises his arm. I'd forgotten what a big man he is.

She's shaking too bad to answer.

"Wasn't nobody naked," Rufe says.

Their daddy's face is red. He doesn't even look toward Rufe. His open hand falls to his side. "I'll see you at home," he tells Charlotte. "Wait for me there."

☼

Charlotte doesn't go home. When I left her, her face was so pale it looked like milk with a couple of light brown freckles floating on top. "I'll be okay," she said. But in the middle of supper, Glad bangs on the door: "Charlotte's mother says come quick!"

He leads me past the Williams house, with Uncle Moody and Aunt Van right behind. The dirt road turns left, and there's a group of people in the woods there: Charlotte's brothers and her mom and dad. They're staring into the branches of a tall tree.

"What's going on?" Uncle Moody asks.

Mrs. Williams is crying. "Charlotte's in the pin oak, and she won't come down." A leather belt dangles from Mr. Williams' hand.

"Evening, Bucky," Uncle Moody says. Mr. Williams doesn't even look our way.

"Charlotte, I'm going to give you one last chance," he yells.

She shouts down, "No!"

"Then I'm sending Jimbo up to get you."

Jimbo's eyes get wide. "Daddy, I can't climb that tree, 'cause I'm scairt of heights."

"Do as I say."

"But, Duke—"

"Go on." His daddy turns sharply. Jimbo puts his hands on the trunk, wipes them on his jeans, puts them back. Though he's strong, he's not agile like

Charlotte. He climbs a few feet. The branches snap like twigs under his worn sneakers. He clings to the tree, doesn't move. After a while he crawls back down.

"Duke!"

But Duke's too smart for that—he's disappeared. There's no one else to go: Sonny's too little, and Rufe can't risk it—if he hits his head again, he could die. Van has her arm around Mrs. Williams. "She'll be all right, Shirley." Charlotte's mom doesn't answer. Mr. Williams grabs the hatchet from Jimbo's belt and takes a couple whacks at the tree trunk, but the blade's so dull it hardly cuts, and he hurls it into the woods and stalks off. We all stand there staring as the back of his undershirt slowly fades into the brush.

"Charlotte," someone calls, "he's gone."

She doesn't answer.

Mrs. Williams keeps on crying. She calls to Charlotte to come down, but there's no reply. She grabs Sonny's hand. "I'm sorry to bother you," she tells us. "I knew you were at supper when I sent that boy. But when Bucky gets upset . . ."

"Don't worry about us," Uncle Moody says. He and Aunt Van walk her and Sonny home. The rest of us stay under the tree, gazing up. All I can see of Charlotte is a thin strip of her bright blue dress.

"You didn't help him, Jimmy," Rufe says. "That was good."

"But I lost my hatchet. I had that hatchet since third grade. I got it for Christmas." Jimbo sounds like he's talking about his teddy bear. He's blinking back tears.

"It's over there in the leaves," Rufe says. "Glad and me'll help you find it, won't we, Glad?"

The three of them start stomping around in the woods. "Come on, Dawn," Rufe calls. "You help, too."

12

The next day Glad brings a message from Charlotte: she's okay, and she'll meet me at the planet around noon. She doesn't say she's bringing Sonny, too. I hear them crashing up the path. When they come around the corner, he's fussing about the blindfold. She yanks it off and shoves him down. He blinks, sees me, blinks again.

"I thought this was outer space, but it can't be if you're here."

"It is."

"Then how'd you get here—on a rocket?" Sonny's cleaner than usual this morning; his tee shirt has a little bit of scrambled egg blended into the cloth, but that's all, and his hair looks like someone actually brushed it.

"I got here like you did—through the magic gate."

He puts his hands on his hips and stares me in the face. "What do you think, Dawn—I'm stupid? There's no such thing as a magic gate."

"Then how'd you get here?"

That sets him back. He starts looking all around. We tell him the same thing we told Glad: it's unexplored, so it's dangerous outside the clearing; and if you talk about it, you'll drop dead. He's lying on the ground looking at some bugs.

"Tell me about last night," I say to Charlotte. She makes herself comfortable. Her eyes are bright.

"After you left, Rufe and Jimbo and Glad kept looking for that hatchet til they found it. Then they hollered they was going home. By then I was getting tired, but I knew I had to hold on until dark.

"Once it did get dark, those woods were awful quiet. I'd hear something in the leaves, but I couldn't see what. I waited and waited, thinking Daddy might come back. Finally my hands and arms got so tired I couldn't wait no more, and I started down. I could see the branches at eye level, but I just had to feel with my feet and knees. Seemed like it took forever before I touched the ground.

"I ran up the road fast as I could. There was lights on in the house, but I knew I wasn't going in. But

Rufe and Duke was waiting by the barn—they'd got an old blanket someplace. They wanted me to sleep down there, but I came here instead."

"You slept at Planet Kid?"

She wags her head toward Sonny, winks at me. "I knew Daddy couldn't find it, 'cause he doesn't know about the gate."

"That makes sense."

"This morning I hid down by the road until his truck went by. Then I went home. Mama was so glad to see me, she started crying."

Charlotte grins, but there's something uneasy behind that smile. Maybe she's worried about tonight.

"Will your dad be mad when he comes home?"

She shakes her head. "He cools down once he sleeps. You just got to stay out of his way for the evening, then the next day say you're sorry."

☼

Sonny loves Planet Kid. He says it's got all new bugs, different from American bugs. He shows me a blue one with black legs. "Ain't that beautiful, Dawn? That's the bestest bug I ever found."

"That's real nice, Sonny."

"You want to hold him?"

"That ain't a him, it's a her." Charlotte peers down

at the bug. "We already told you, what's on Planet Kid is girls."

Sonny looks disgusted. "I don't like girls. They got cooties."

"What do you think we are, dummy?"

He seems surprised, like he never thought of that before.

☼

Later Glad shows up. I'm sitting on the glider, looking at *Sports Illustrated*, when he plops himself down beside me without a word. Little while later, he says, "Let's play the piano."

We go in and sit on the bench. As usual, Aunt Van's in the kitchen. I start off with "Take Me Out to the Ball Game," playing it as loud as I can. Glad watches my hands, then picks out the melody, adding a few lines of bass. "Go ahead," I say, kidding around. "Do something else." He plays the C-scale then, and after that, "Chopsticks."

By now I'm getting mad. After all my practicing, how can he play better than me? I do the hardest song I know, a minuet by Mozart. I miss some notes here and there, but it sounds sort of like it's supposed to. But Glad shakes his head. "I heard that on the radio," he whispers. "It should be soft."

"You do it then, if you're so smart."

"Show me w-w-w-where it starts."

I don't feel like it, but I do. Would you believe he plays it good? Naturally Aunt Van hears, too. "That's so much better, Dawn," she calls. "It's just like day and night, the way you're improving."

"Thanks," I say. Then I slide off the bench and head for Charlotte's, with Glad tagging after me.

☼

Her dad's not home, and all five kids are outdoors playing hide-and-seek. Charlotte calls it car hide-and-seek, 'cause where they hide's mostly in the old cars spread across the yard. They're yelling at each other— "I got you! You know I tagged you first!" When they see Glad and me they shout for us to play. It's like yesterday never even happened. Jimbo's *it*: I hide in the backseat of an old Chevy. I can see where mice pulled some of the stuffing out to make a nest. His boots crunch past on the grass. Then he finds somebody. There's screams and wild laughter. "You're *it*! You're *it*!" The rest of us come out. Charlotte hides her face and starts counting.

This time I hide in the toolshed by the porch. I'm peeking out the door when Mrs. Williams comes to take the laundry off the line. She passes within three feet of me, but she doesn't know I'm here. There's something a little different about the way she looks. I study her face from behind the door. For the first time I can remember she's wearing makeup, so that her skin seems pinker and smoother than usual, but even so there's a dark spot under her right eye. "Here I come, ready or not!" Charlotte calls. I pull the shed door closed.

13

Lying on the glider on the front porch, I make believe I meet the Senators' best pitcher, Camilo Pascual. I'm pitching with my hair tucked in my hat. He sees me and comes up to talk. He's Cuban, so he has an accent:

"What's your name, boy?"

"Dawn."

"Don, let me see that curve again."

I rear back and throw it: *zing!*

"Do it again." (Maybe he thought the last one was just luck.)

This time I put a topspin on the ball, and it breaks the other way. He shakes his head, stares down at me. "How old are you?"

"I turned twelve in May."

"You like the Senators?"

"That's the only team I want to play for."

He puts his hand out, and we shake. He turns as he's leaving: "What was that name?"

"Dawn Wesley." I take my hat off. My hair spills all around my shoulders. He stares.

"I don't believe it," he says softly.

※

Charlotte's in a bad mood. When I ask her to play, she glares at me like I'm useless: "I got to help Ma scrub the kitchen. Darn pissants came through the wall and got into the cupboard. They were in the sugar bowl when Daddy made his coffee."

"What're pissants?"

"You don't know what pissants are? Dawn, what grade are you in, anyway?"

I start to ask her why she's mad, but she goes on: "Maybe they don't have pissants in Washington. Maybe the only ones that got pissants is us hill-billies."

"What's the matter with you, Charlotte?"

"Nothing's the matter with me." She mimics my voice.

My feelings are hurt, but something inside won't let me give up asking what I want to know.

"Why don't you use bug spray? Then you wouldn't have to scrub all day."

She's glaring. "You don't get it, do you, Dawn?"

"What?"

"We got to do what he tells us." She's on her knees now on the worn linoleum floor, a rag in her hand, a bucket of soapy water beside her.

"How come?"

"What do you think?"

"I don't know what to think."

But when I walk away from there, my heart is pounding.

14

When I try to talk to Charlotte about yesterday, she brushes it off: "I was just upset, that's all. It's not your business, anyway."

"But you shouldn't be afraid of your own dad."

"I'm not afraid, okay?" She's getting mad again. "Listen, I came down here to tell you something. . . ."

She's got another plan to trick the boys. She shows me a pair of black plastic trash bags, then slides one on over her dress. "Look, Dawn!" There're holes cut in the top for eyes. "And I've got black socks and my old patent leather shoes. You've got dark stuff, don't you?"

"Yeah." But right away I'm nervous. It was just luck Moody and Van didn't find out about that day I went fishing without permission.

Charlotte's not worried about getting in trouble. She nods happily. "Here's exactly what we're going to do."

My first part in her scheme is to bring Glad to the planet. But he won't come unless I call him by a new name: Alec. I saw him with a book a couple days ago: *The Black Stallion*.

"The hero's Alec, isn't he?"

His eyes light up. "Alec Ramsay."

"At Planet Kid we got wild horses, too. Want me to take you there? We might not see them—sometimes they're on the other side of the mountain—but we might."

We're in the barn when I tell him this. Alec pats Star, rubs her forehead. She leans into it, so you can tell she's happy.

"Can she come?"

"No, it's too far, and she doesn't like the blindfold, either."

Alec looks disappointed, but he follows me.

✵

Charlotte's gone ahead, like she planned. When I lead Alec into Planet Kid, there's a note tied to the stem of a jimsonweed: FOR BOYS ONLY. I take off his blindfold, and he grabs it right away.

"Let me see!"

But he shakes his head. He turns away, reads it,

turns back smiling. He folds the note and sticks it in his pocket.

☼

A minute later Charlotte comes, leading Sonny. They're singing "Wake Up Little Susie," and trying to jitterbug. Sonny's tripping over his own two feet, 'cause he can't see. Charlotte takes the blindfold off and winks at me: "What you doing tonight, Dawn?"

"Got to stay at home and write a letter to my mom."

"I'm going over Cheryl Anne Beasley's. She goes to our church, and she passed a message from her daddy to mine that she wants to see me. She's got new paper dolls, and she wants me to help her cut them out. We might make some sugar cookies, too."

I happen to know Charlotte can't stand Cheryl Anne Beasley, but I keep my mouth shut.

"Can I go?" Sonny whines.

"Course not. This is girl stuff."

"I don't get to do nothing." He plops down on the ground and manages to get a tear started in one eye. Alec's watching him, then he pulls on his sleeve and they whisper. When they look up, Sonny's grinning. "I got something to do my own self," he tells us.

"What?" Charlotte asks.

But Alec puts one finger to his mouth, and for a miracle, Sonny doesn't tell.

☆

Later we see Rufe walking with Alec. The two of them are grinning and rubbing their hands together, so we know they're hooked. Then Charlotte stuffs a feedbag with straw. She puts some trash in and some Pepsi bottles filled with muddy water from the creek. All this time I'm watching, wondering how this will turn out.

"Here's what the note said—" She's excited now. "There's a sack of candy and pop in the clearing past the Williamses' barn; but you must go at midnight."

"What if they bring flashlights?" I'm looking for a reason to back out.

She shakes her head. "They can't. We ain't got no batteries."

"Maybe *we'll* get scared, down there in the dark."

She looks at me like I'm stupid, and she says, "What are you, Dawn, a baby?"

☆

It's late when I sneak down the back-hall stairs. Once I'm outside, I take off for the barn; Charlotte's there, and she helps me get dressed. We tie strings around our foreheads to keep the plastic bags in place. Charlotte surveys me carefully, then looks herself over. "I guess we'll pass," she says cheerfully. "Follow me."

We trudge down the hill to the road. There's hardly any moon. I'd forgotten about all those years when I had a night-light in my room in the apartment: one in the hall, and the bathroom, too. When we cut through the fencerow toward the woods, I feel a shiver in my spine.

"Charlotte?"

"Yeah?" She doesn't even slow down.

"Uhhhh. . . ."

"Hurry up, Dawn," she says.

☼

She's left the burlap bag behind a tree. We drag it to a stump in the middle of the clearing. The bottles are on top. In the dark, though, there's barely a glint of light from the glass; and I wonder if they'll find the sack at all. Charlotte's confident. "Soon as they get to it, we'll jump up and start moaning. Then they'll tear off screaming, just you wait and see."

We hide behind a honeysuckle thicket. Seems like we wait forever. Neither of us has a watch, so we don't even know what time it is. I'm getting cramps in my legs from squatting there. I keep shifting position, but nothing helps. I'm so tired I feel like falling asleep right on the ground. Then—finally—we hear a crackle in the brush. There're whispers, low and breathless, but I can't tell what they're saying. Charlotte sticks her head out to the side.

"It's them! I see Alec and Sonny and Rufe!"

I stick my head around and peep out, too. Rufe's out front, with Alec and Sonny behind him. The little boys are so close together, they look like Siamese twins. I think I hear Sonny's teeth chattering in the dark. There's the sound of their voices, twigs crackling; but from behind them there's more noise, and I notice suddenly, two other shapes.

"Charlotte?"

"Huh?"

"I think there's someone else. . . ."

She looks again. "Uh-oh," she says.

"What?"

"They brought Jimbo; Duke, too." She shifts slightly in the thicket, puts her hand up to her mouth. "Dawn," she whispers, "Duke don't go nowhere at night without his gun."

It's us that's shaking now. We watch them search, hoping they don't see anything. But they won't give up; they circle the clearing, passing right in front of us. Rufe says, "It's got to be here somewhere." Charlotte and I cling to each other.

When they finally spot the bag, Duke goes up first. There's a murmur of voices, laughter. I see the butt of his rifle sticking out behind him. I whisper, "Let's stand up now. We can tell them it was all a joke."

"No, Dawn!" She's crouched there, frozen. Duke picks up one of the Pepsi bottles, raises it to his mouth. He spits onto the ground, cusses. He wheels around, shouting.

"We got to run, Dawn!" Charlotte whispers. Before I can stop her she's on her feet.

The boys don't see her til she starts to move. I don't know who screams first, but it's loud, so loud and scary that I find myself screaming, too, without even knowing it. The boys are tearing toward the Williamses' house. The gun goes off; I don't know how Duke aimed, whether he even saw us in the dark. A minute later they're gone.

I get slowly to my feet. After a while I see her. She's lying in a bush, her church shoes tangled in the vines. I go over there slow, and she looks up.

"Ch-ch-charlotte? Y-y-y-you ok-k-k-kay?"

She doesn't answer right away; then she nods and says, in a tiny voice, "You sound just like Alec."

·☼·

That whole night is just plain rough. Soon as I get inside the kitchen door, Uncle Moody's there: "Where you been, Dawn? I didn't hear you ask permission to go nowhere." Then he adds, "Why are you wearing a plastic bag?"

I can't decide whether to tell or keep quiet. He's in a bad mood.

"I don't know about Washington, but in Sturvis County, Virginia, girls don't go wandering around in the middle of the night." His voice is gruff. "And sneaking out, too. Miss, one of these days your behavior's going to get you a spanking."

I start crying. "Please don't spank me, Uncle Moody. I'll never be bad again, I swear."

He looks upset, too. "I don't want to spank you . . . ," he begins. "But . . ."

"I want to go home!" This idea comes out of nowhere. I cry as hard as I can: boo-hoo-hoo. Suddenly I *do* want to go home. I'm worried about Charlotte's dad, and I don't know what to do. I miss Mom, too. It's been so long since I've even seen her. I think of how her neck smelled when I was little and she held me in her lap: warm and perfumey and alive. Then I sit at the kitchen table and cry and cry.

15

Next day, Mom calls. She must have talked to Van and Moody first, 'cause she asks about last night.

"Why did you do that, Dawn? Why did you sneak out without asking?"

I'm silent for a minute. "No reason, really."

"Were you meeting Charlotte?"

I don't answer, 'cause I might get her in trouble, too.

"'Cause if you were, you two need to do your pranking during daylight hours. Moody said they didn't have the faintest idea where you were, or what you were doing. Then a gun went off, and they were scared to death."

"I'm sorry."

"You need to tell them that." She's quiet, too. Then, almost as if she can read my mind, she asks, "Is everything okay?"

I want to tell her about Charlotte, but I know how

sick she's been, and how she's working to get well. *"This summer, you're on your own,"* Daddy'd said.

"No . . . that is . . . Mom?"

"What, sweetie?"

I almost tell, then I change my mind and think of something fast. "I might trade some of my baseball cards. I'd mail them to Mr. Hooper at the shop. Is that okay?"

"Of course, it is." She sounds surprised. "You bought the cards—they're yours to do with as you please." She waits a minute. "You'll see him in less than a month, you know, 'cause you'll be home. Then you can walk to the hobby shop every day. . . ."

"Less than a month?" I don't want to say how long that sounds.

☼

Aunt Van calls me from the yard. She's heading into Lynville for groceries, and after last night's escapade, she doesn't want to leave me here alone.

"And Charlotte?"

She sighs. "I'd like to know where Charlotte was last night."

"Charlotte had nothing to do with it. I just wanted to look at the stars."

She looks at me doubtfully. "You wore a trash bag to see the stars?"

I can't think of what to say.

Aunt Van sighs again. "Run ask her, quick."

⚛

Charlotte, who's been to Lynville a million times, calls it Podunk Central. But there's a supermarket, a drugstore, and a five-and-dime filled with long wooden tables. One is marked five cents, another ten, and the one near the back says a quarter. Whatever's on there, you can have it for that price. Charlotte and I start by pawing through the nickel table. She finds some hair bands and a bag of balloons. We grab magic slates and colored chalk. Our total comes to sixty cents, but Aunt Van gave us each a dollar, so we add a pack of M&M's. There's still enough money to get ice creams at the drugstore.

Afterwards, we take our loot to the supermarket. Aunt Van is poised in front of the cereal row. "Oatmeal or Cream of Wheat?" she asks. I beg for sugar-frosted flakes, but Uncle Moody says they taste like candied leaves, so she buys Wheaties instead. Ted Williams smiles from the front of the box. Charlotte thumps him on the chest with her finger, teasing me. Aunt Van throws a pound of coffee and a bag of oranges into the cart before we pay up.

Then we load our groceries into the station wagon and drive three blocks to Southern States Co-op.

Uncle Moody's behind the counter. He didn't know we were coming by, and his face flushes with pleasure. Red's lying in the corner; he gets up and licks Charlotte and me on the legs. She giggles and squirms, but I squat down and pat his head the way he likes.

"Got ducklings in the back, girls." Uncle Moody points off to the right.

"Oh!" We run through to the feed bay. Sheltered from the open platform, back behind the shelves of nutrition supplement and bone meal, is a cage filled with flapping yellow fuzz balls. We get down on our knees, reach in, and take out one apiece. The baby ducks squeal and croak. Their orange feet tread air as they try to escape. "Mine's named Herman," Charlotte says.

"And mine's . . . Camilo."

"Camilo? What's that?"

"Just a name I heard somewhere."

We keep on playing with the ducklings til Aunt Van says we have to go.

☼

Later we troop over to the planet and spend time fixing it up: rearranging the pillows, setting up some scraps of board for shelves. We pick daisies and stick them in a Pepsi bottle filled with water from the creek. Then we lie with our heads on the burlap sacks, staring up into the sky.

"Did you get caught sneaking in last night?" I ask Charlotte.

She shakes her head. "The boys were sleeping down under the oak tree, Alec, too, so I was the only one had to get in and out. I walked on my tiptoes, let me tell you, girl. I can shut that screen door quieter than you would believe."

"Uncle Moody was at the kitchen table when I came in. Said if I do something like that again, I'll get a spanking."

Charlotte's not too sympathetic. "I'm surprised he didn't stripe your legs right then and there."

"What's that?"

"What?"

"To stripe your legs . . ."

She raises her head onto her elbow to stare at me. "You never got black-and-blue marks from a whipping?"

"I've never been spanked."

"You're lying."

"No, I'm not."

She sits up now, looks me in the eye. "What happens when you're bad?"

"I get sent to my room. Sometimes they take away something I like, like listening to the ball game."

"That's *all*?" She acts like she can't believe her ears. "My daddy'll whip your tail for sneezing, if he's in the mood."

"For sneezing?" I try to treat it like a joke.

"For anything. Last night he beat on Jimbo for eating two pork chops, 'cause that's gluttony. Ma and Rufe told him to stop, but then he said he'd hurt them, too."

Suddenly I remember the marks on Rufe's back, and what they'd said to Mr. Williams in the hospital. "I thought he wasn't s'posed to hit Rufe anymore."

"Once he gets riled up, Ma says there's naught but God can stop him. And God won't." Charlotte looks sad. "It's in the Bible, Dawn—'Spare the rod and spoil the child.' "

I think of Timmy, who has a habit of taking cookies without asking. "Your mom doesn't believe that, does she?"

"She cries, if one of us gets whipped, and sometimes she'll try to make him stop. But later she says the Word of God's supreme o'er all."

I remember the dark spot on her face, that day when we were playing hide-and-seek. "He hits her, too, doesn't he?"

"Sometimes," Charlotte says. She's on her back again, staring into the sky. "He says it's so she'll be a good wife, and obey."

Later she says, "I'm never getting married, Dawn."

"No," I say. "Me neither."

16

We think the boys don't know who tricked them, but they do. It might have something to do with Charlotte leaving her trash bag, socks, *and* shoes in a heap beside the Williamses' back door. But they don't mention it directly: instead I find a paper taped on the barn wall, near my pitching target. I take it down and open it. The message is printed in block letters:

YOU WILL PAY

"We won't either," Charlotte says, laughing. "We ain't got no money, do we, Dawn?"

"Maybe they're not talking about money."

"How else can you pay?"

"I don't know."

☼

But it turns out I'm right. The next day, when we get to Planet Kid, it looks like a whirlwind hit it: shelves broken, jimsonweed hacked up, pillows torn, and the straw scattered everywhere. The Pepsi-bottle vase and the mason jar that held our drinking water are smashed. Even the books are shredded, like someone had a giant temper fit and ripped out pages one by one. At first I don't make the connection. "Who would do this? Why?" Tears are rolling down my cheeks.

"We'll fix it back," Charlotte says. "And then we'll get them good."

"Get who?"

"Who do you think, dummy? Remember the note?"

It hits me then. "Those creeps!" I stomp around, then plop down on the ground. "Those stupid creeps!"

"I told you they were bad."

"I can't believe they did this! And Alec—was he part of it?"

"Probably. He's been hanging around with Rufe and Sonny. Yesterday they were over at his place watching TV."

I'm getting madder and madder. "I'm going to get them back."

"How, Dawn?"

"I'll tell Uncle Moody. He'll punish them, I know."

"He might tell Daddy." Her mood changes. Now she reminds me of her mom—nervous but down to earth. "It won't be hard to fix this place back up," she says, looking around. "Let's do it now. When we're finished, we can figure out our own revenge."

"Why should we have to clean it up? We didn't make this mess!"

"No, but it won't be hard to fix up, either. Come on, let's get started."

☼

She's right. We rake up the broken glass, fetch new feedsacks and straw, new boards, another jar and Pepsi bottle. We set things back the way they were. The planet looks pretty good—it's actually a little bigger than it was before, 'cause the boys hacked down more weeds. But the books can't be replaced.

"This Nancy Drew was one of my best, *The Hidden Staircase*. And this other one I got for my birthday two years ago. Mom gave it to me."

"When's your birthday?"

"May nineteen."

"You were twelve, right? What did you get?"

"I don't remember—" I do really, but I won't tell Charlotte: a Wilson baseball glove, the Don Larsen model.

"I won't be twelve til February. By then the money's usually gone, 'cause of Christmas . . ."

"What'd you get last year?"

"Ma sewed me a pretty coat, blue with pink lining. I wore it Easter Day. Then Sonny left some Crayolas on it, and they melted, and we couldn't get the wax out, so it's stained."

I feel bad for her, only getting clothes; but I say, "That's neat your mom can sew. I hate going to the store and trying things on."

"There ain't much *to* try on, at Podunk Central." She grins suddenly, as if she's back on track. "Maybe one day you'll invite me to the city, and I'll come on the Greyhound bus. Then we can go shopping."

"That would be nice—real nice." But secretly I wonder what it would be like. What would Charlotte think of our apartment, with its modern furniture and bright red rugs? Would she laugh at Mr. Hooper's messy hobby shop? Would she understand that kids can't go out alone at night?

☼

Later I practice the piano. I'm rusty, since Alec's been doing it for me; and some of the songs I thought I had down pat come out ragged. My fingers aren't hitting the right keys. I try "Onward, Christian Soldiers." Aunt Van comes to the door and stares. I turn red.

"I'm having a bad day."

She smiles then. "That happens to everyone. I remember sometimes Evie'd get so frustrated with her sketching, she'd sit in this same room, Dawn, and tear the paper into bits. She'd swear that she was never going to draw again. But the next day she'd be right back at it."

I don't say anything, but I'm thinking, *At least she didn't have someone else drawing for her.*

I try "America." Uncle Moody takes his coffee and the newspaper, and goes and sits on the front porch.

17

Star's sick. She doesn't raise her head when I come in, and her breathing is so strained her sides look like a fireplace bellows. Uncle Moody calls the vet to look at her.

Star is Mom's pony. Moody and Van bought her shortly after Mom came to the farm. Star was a foal then, and Mom raised her, feeding her bottle after bottle, bathing her coat with horse shampoo, cleaning her tiny hooves and polishing them with stoveblack til they shone.

When Star was two, Mom gentled her to the saddle and bridle. After that she rode her every day. Aunt Van took pictures. I've seen those photographs—Mom and Star look as close as a person and an animal could ever be. Remembering that, I sigh. "Mom will be here in a couple of weeks," I tell Star. She looks at me as if she understands.

Charlotte's not home. Turns out Mrs. Tucker needed someone to help her in the kitchen, cleaning out her cupboards, and Mr. Williams told her Charlotte would. She'll be gone for the whole day. "But she's getting paid," her mom says proudly. "Twenty cents an hour, Dawn. Isn't that great?"

"I guess." I wander back across the yard. Rufe and Alec are sitting in a rusted Chevy, facing the field. Rufe's got his hands on the wheel, turning it back and forth. After a while I knock on the back fender. Rufe looks in the rearview mirror, sees me, cranks down the window.

"Hey, Dawn."

"Hey."

"What you doing?"

"Nothing." I shift from foot to foot. He's watching like he knows what's going on.

"Somebody tore our place up, this place we had out in the jimsonweeds. I reckon they were mad at us for something else."

"Like what?" Rufe asks. He isn't smiling, but he doesn't look mad either.

"Like putting a bag of trash out in the woods and pretending it was candy. Whoever did that—one of them never wanted to, and she's sorry about it now."

All the time I'm making this speech Alec doesn't look at me, so I *know* he's mad. I try the back-door handle, but it's locked. Rufe turns and lifts the plastic knob. There's a smell of cat pee in the backseat.

"Yuck." I have to hold my nose to keep from gagging. "Why'd you pick this car?"

"Alec's daddy has a Chevy."

Suddenly I remember that car beside the house the time Charlotte and I hid under the window. "Where's your dad now, Alec?"

He's staring out the front. He doesn't answer.

"You ain't talking to her, little buddy?" Rufe puts his arm over the back of the seat.

"She lies," Alec says.

My face turns red. "It was just a stupid joke."

"And Planet Kid?"

"What about it?" But I'm getting redder and redder. It feels like any minute my skin's going to crawl right off my face.

He stares at me for a minute, then turns to Rufe as if I didn't exist. "Let's go to California."

"We're on our way," Rufe says cheerfully. I hear his foot tapping the gas pedal, then he steers and pretends to honk the horn. They don't speak to me. But I'm not getting out, not yet, anyway. I sit scowling in the back.

"Think I see the ocean, little buddy," Rufe says. "Hear them waves?"

Alec nods.

"See them surfers?"

"Yep."

"Want to go to Disneyland?"

"Oh, yeah!" Alec doesn't even stutter.

"Disneyland costs money," I object. "You can't go there unless you're rich."

But they ignore me, keep on smiling and talking to each other like they're on vacation and I'm a piece of lint on one of the backseat cushions. I try to come up with some pleasant conversation: "What kind of fools would ride all the way to California in a car that stinks like pee?"

They don't answer. Rufe turns the dial on the radio, starts singing "Rock Around the Clock" in a high squeaky voice. Then he tells the weather: "For the state of California, we have temperatures in the mid-eighties, perfect for swimming. Have a wonderful day."

"I'm not having a wonderful day!" I shout. They turn.

"How come?" Rufe asks finally.

"Star's sick. Uncle Moody called the vet, 'cause she can't breathe. She didn't even eat her oats."

They think it's just another story, like Planet Kid.

I burst into tears. "Do you think I'd lie about Star?" Rufe's eyes soften then.

"Don't cry, Dawn," he says. "We'll drive over and have a look-see—when we get back from California, that is."

Now that I've started crying, I can't stop. "She's *real* sick . . ."

"We'll be over, won't we, little buddy?"

Alec nods, but he doesn't look at me.

☼

The vet comes after supper. By then everybody knows Star's sick. They're quiet and serious, standing back: Charlotte and Sonny, Alec, Rufe, and Jimbo, too. I stay by Uncle Moody, 'cause I'm family. The vet crouches next to Star, listens to her breathing and her heart. He pats her with one hand, "Take it easy, young lady"; but her ears flatten against her head, as if she remembers him. After he gets up, he gestures to Moody. They stand in the far corner of the stall, talking in low voices. "There's a chance . . . " I see Uncle Moody's lips move, try to make out what he says. The vet squats down, gives Star a shot.

"Time to go, kids," Uncle Moody says. "It's bedtime now."

Rufe answers, "Mr. Moody, we ain't gone to bed at eight o'clock since we was nine years old, probably not even then."

He smiles, but his face looks longer than usual. Charlotte, Alec, and Sonny are playing with the cat. "How is she anyway?" Rufe asks.

"Not so hot." Uncle Moody speaks low, so the little kids won't hear.

Jimbo keeps on smiling, but Rufe looks stunned. Uncle Moody puts his hand on Rufe's shoulder. "It's age, son. Her heart's not pumping like it's s'posed to."

Jimbo's smile drains off, and his round face sags. "Star might die?"

"That's what he said, Jimmy."

"Ain't no pills he can give her?"

"Pills won't work." Uncle Moody doesn't notice me standing behind Rufe. "Don't y'all say nothing to them youngsters, hear?"

"You mean she's *bound* to die?" Jimbo has tears in his eyes. I'm not sure, but it looks like Uncle Moody might, too. He clears his throat, but the words rattle like a bad cough.

"He's got some shots to give her, but he thinks she's slid too far. We all got to go sometime, you know."

"She's the only pony I ever rode." Tears spill out and roll down Jimbo's cheeks. They're streaking my face, too.

"Tears you up, don't it?" Uncle Moody shakes his head before he goes up to the house.

18

But Star makes it through the night, and in the morning she seems to be breathing a little easier. I don't pitch, because the noise might bother her. Instead I practice the piano like crazy: "Onward, Christian Soldiers," "The Old Rugged Cross," "Jesus Loves Me!" Finally Aunt Van comes from the kitchen: "That's enough, Dawn. I can hardly hear myself think."

I sit with her while she starts the pot roast that we'll have for supper. She puts on the radio: "Blue Suede Shoes." Her feet are tapping, and her arms move to the rhythm as she peels carrots and potatoes. "I wish they'd had this music when I was young. I could have cut a rug on this." She smiles. "That's what we used to call fast dancing."

"How'd you learn to dance, anyway?"

"Ina taught me, when I was just your age." Ina was Van's sister, my mom's mother. "We learned the jitterbug, the Charleston, all the old dances. My daddy didn't approve, so we had to sneak out to the dance hall. The night he caught us, there was holy heck in our house."

"Did he stripe your legs?"

She looks surprised. "No, we were too old for that, honey. But he wouldn't let us out again no matter what boy came around. If I wanted to see Moody, I had to haul milk cans to the dairy in town, then I'd stop by his porch on my way home."

"What did he look like then?"

"He was handsome—the best-looking boy in Lynville." Her eyes brighten, remembering. "Ina teased me—'You're not falling for a farm boy, are you Vanessa? I thought we agreed we'd go to college.' My daddy didn't want to hear about Moody, either. But Moody had two good hunting dogs, so before he ever mentioned my name, he arranged to take Daddy quail hunting. Then after they'd bagged a few, they got around to talking about me."

"How long have you been married?"

"Forty years, come November nine. We've had our rough times, but all around it's worked out good."

"During your rough times . . ." I'm not sure how to ask, so I just blurt it out: "Does Uncle Moody hit you?"

"Heavens, no!" Aunt Van stares at me like I'm a stranger. "What in the world put that into your head?"

I hesitate, knowing that Charlotte will be mad at me, then plunge ahead: "Bucky Williams hits his wife."

"Where'd you hear that?" Aunt Van's still staring, and she sounds upset.

"Charlotte. And once, I saw a bruise on Mrs. Williams' cheek, right here."

"Oh, mercy, child, she could have done anything—banged her face on the mop handle, for all you know. And Charlotte has a wild imagination. You shouldn't jump to conclusions, Dawn."

"I'm not." I put my hands in front of me on the table, turn them over like I'm about to pick up a ball and throw it. "He hits his kids, too."

"It's different from where you live, isn't it?" Aunt Van's voice is kind. "Around here, most people spank their children. Parents have to maintain standards, you know, honey. If they didn't spank their kids when they did wrong, the kids wouldn't *know* right from wrong."

"Spare the rod and spoil the child—"

"Yes, that's in the Good Book." She nods. "Moody and I didn't follow it, though. I spanked Evie once or twice, but it only seemed to make her mad. She said Moody and I were bullies, and she wouldn't do a thing we told her to. One night we got down on our knees and prayed for guidance. Moody heard the

Lord say, 'Patience'; so we followed that. But there were times when I was sorely tried."

"What's that?"

She laughs. "It means I was tempted. Dawn, you can't even *imagine* how naughty that child was."

"Mom?"

"Oh, honey." She puts her face between her hands, shakes her head, looks up smiling. "*You* don't know the meaning of bad, compared to Evie."

"I don't?"

"No. That child was orneriness itself. Why, she'd sit at this table and refuse to eat because we wouldn't let the dog sleep in her bed. Said she'd starve herself to death if we didn't let her. Then she refused to change her socks for two straight weeks. Another time she told the teacher to go you-know-where, and when we tried to get her to apologize, she told us to go right straight to the same place."

I can't believe what I'm hearing. "What did you do?"

"I don't remember everything we tried, but nothing worked. She'd get this certain expression, and I'd know right then and there the situation was hopeless."

I picture Mom and make a face. "It's like this, isn't it?"

She smiles. "That's it exactly!"

"Mom got that look when she decided to get the operation. Dad and I wanted her to wait, but her mind was made up."

Aunt Van nods. "That stubbornness can be a good thing, too—it can take you through hard times. And Evie had her share of those, being orphaned like she was. She was a child who carried a load of sorrow."

The phone sounds then—two shorts and one long, the farm's code. Aunt Van picks it up. "Hi, Sharon." She smiles, and I know our conversation's over. I wander out, feeling confused. Why didn't she listen when I told her about Charlotte's dad? Back in Washington, men get put in jail for beating each other up. Is beating your family different from that? Is hitting children actually okay?

☼

Around here, all the phones are on a party line, which means that you can pick up the receiver and eavesdrop on someone's conversation, if you're quiet. Charlotte's done this a million times—so much that she hardly even enjoys it anymore. She says she knows everybody's business, and it's flat-out boring. But lately she's out of touch, because the Williams lost their phone a couple months ago. "They took it out because we couldn't pay the bill," she says matter-of-factly.

"We'll probably get it back at haying, when the boys can make some extra money."

In the meantime, she has to do her eavesdropping on other people's phones. She giggles when she tells me how she listened in at Mrs. Tucker's. "See, Dawn, they have a phone right there in the kitchen, so naturally, when she went out, I picked it up to see if anyone was talking. You won't believe what I heard!"

"What?"

"I heard Duke!" She's whispering, 'cause we're up in her room, lying on the bed, and in her house, you never know who's spying.

"Who was he talking to?"

"A woman. She was asking him questions, like when he turned eighteen, what he studied in school, and what kind of stuff he likes to read."

It's hard for me to imagine any of the Williams in a classroom or reading books. "You said your brothers are dumb."

"They are! But Duke's school-smart, know what I mean? He's even got some books under his bed. He got them from the school librarian, 'cause they were going to throw them out."

We toss the questions back and forth: Who was Duke talking to? Whose phone was he using? What were he and the woman talking about?

"Did she sound like a girlfriend?"

"She didn't call him honey or darling or nothing like that."

"Could she have been from the high school?"

"No, because a teacher would have known that stuff."

"Did he mention talking to anyone?"

"He ain't said nothing to us," Charlotte says. "So whatever it is, it's secret."

"Not for long," I murmur, and she grins.

19

My dad sends clippings from the *Washington Post*. I unfold them and spread them across my knees:

PASCUAL PITCHES SHUTOUT NUMBER 5
NINTH-INNING HOMER WINS FOR SENATORS
RAMOS BEATS YANKS IN 12

He's written comments on each page. There's a note attached, too, on stationery from one of the galleries where he works:

Hope you heard these on the radio, Dawn—Great games! Mom and I were listening from Baltimore. We ate the local specialty—steamed crabs. I got the recipe, so I can make a batch when we get home.

Mom's getting around better now. Today she made it all the way down the corridor and back. . . .

Alec comes looking for me. He's not mad anymore, so we go to Planet Kid to talk. He says, "You don't have to put the blindfold on, 'cause I kn-kn-know it's in the jimsonw-w-weeds."

Turns out he's worried about Charlotte, too. In fact, he brings it up himself: "You know Rufe and them's daddy?" Alec's looking at his shoe. It's a P.F. Flyer, red, with white around the sole. He fingers a place where the rubber trim is loose. "He hits them," he says.

"How do you know?"

"They got bruises." He gestures up and down his front. "Even Sonny. He says he fell, but Gramma told me one time when she w-w-walked past there, their dad was tearing those kids up."

Alec looks up now. I'm sitting still. Here I've been wondering what to do, and so has he. I tell him about my talk with Van, how she said that things are different here.

That's when I ask him, "Do you get spanked?"

"Once, w-w-w-when I ran into the street. Dad said I could have been hit by a car, and killed."

"That's it?"

He nods. "Usually they yell, if I do something bad."

"Yeah, my folks do that, too. Then they send me to my room."

He looks surprised. "W-w-w-what for?"

"For picking on my brother. But they don't see the stuff he does to me."

"My sister's like that, too. She makes it seem like things are all my fault."

I didn't know Alec had a sister. "How old is she?"

"Thirteen. She's called Carrie." His eyes change when he says her name.

I tease him: "You miss her, don't you?"

He shakes his head like he's got bugs on him.

"Will you be glad to see her, when they come for you?"

He won't look at me. "N-n-not *very* glad . . ."

"I miss Timmy and Beth a little, too, even though they're such a pain. This summer, my mom was in the hospital, so they split us up." I tell him about Mom's sickness, and the operation. Alec's a better listener than I thought. Then he tells me how he didn't want to come here, but his father made him, 'cause he thought the country air would do him good.

"I thought the kids round here w-w-would laugh at me, because I stutter. So I tried to spy on you, to see w-w-what you w-w-were like."

"You don't stutter that much—just certain sounds."

He looks pleased when I say that.

"And anyway, I'm not a country kid. I'm from Washington, like you!" We both laugh. The weed pods rustle above our heads. I think for a minute someone's coming, then I see that way high up, the wind's so strong it's blowing the wispy clouds like milkweed seeds. I show Alec, and we lie there watching them.

20

Later we go back to the house so we can practice the piano. Aunt Van's in the garden, weeding tomato plants. When we're done, and Alec and I come out on the porch, she turns and looks at us. Her housedress is sticking to her back.

"Aunt Van?"

"What, honey?" Her voice sounds tired. I feel guilty because of the piano trick. One of these days—maybe today—I'm going to have to tell her. Now I run and get the water pitcher from the refrigerator, fill a tall glass and hurry outside. By the time I get there some of it's splashed out, but she drinks what's left. "Thank you, Dawn."

"You know Alec?"

"You mean Delbert, right?"

"There's something special about him."

"There is?" She looks at me curiously. "What?"

"Uh . . . he's from Washington, same as me."

"Oh."

"See you later."

She shakes her head, frowns, goes back to work.

☼

We visit Star. She's still bad off; the vet comes every day to give her shots. But she whinnies when she sees us. I fetch a handful of oats from the bin and hold them out for her to chew. Her mouth feels good against my hand.

I still can't throw the ball against the barn because of Star. Alec thinks Jimbo or Rufe might play catch with me. I have him ask, 'cause I'm embarrassed; he runs down there and hurries back: "Rufe says come now!" I get my glove and ball and go on down.

Rufe's glove looks like it's from the beginning of baseball: it's flat and thick, with round fat fingers. He hardly says anything to me, just goes and squats out in the field beside their barn. Most of it's high grass, but I can see where the dirt's worn into base paths, as if they used to play ball here.

Rufe's not a bad catcher, though his knees stick out like prongs on a slingshot. He flashes me fake signals, and I nod my head and throw whatever I want.

Whap! The ball smacks leather. When I'm halfway through, Rufe stands up and takes his glove off. He saunters out toward me.

"You're getting my hand sore." He's rubbing it with the other one. His forearm's covered with gold hair and freckles, but his catching hand is pink. "That's fine, when you're throwing at the wall, but I'm a human bein'. You don't want to hurt me, do you?"

"No."

"Okay, then."

He goes back to the spot behind home plate, but before he even crouches down, Jimbo appears. "What you doin', Rufe?"

"Playing catch."

"Let me play."

"Here." He hands Jimbo the glove. "Careful, Jimmy, she throws hard."

"Not too hard for me." But after a minute Jimbo's cussing and holding his hand, too. "Why you got to throw so hard?"

"'Cause I want to pitch in the big leagues."

Jimbo frowns. "I don't think they let no girls in there."

"Maybe I'll be the first."

"Yeah, then you can get me and Rufe on to the Red Sox. That's where we want to play, right, Rufe?"

"That's right, Jimmy." Rufe throws back his head and laughs, like *he* knows it won't really happen, but he doesn't care. "Out there in the outfield with Ted Williams—all three Williams, just like family."

"You should play for the Senators," I say.

They're both laughing now. "No, we want to be with Ted."

Later I keep that picture in my mind, the two of them out in the tall grass, laughing, with sunshine all around.

21

"What're you going to name your children?" Charlotte asks.

We're at Planet Kid. Charlotte's tied Sonny's ankle to a piece of cinderblock, 'cause this morning he went looking for their cow and didn't come back. Everybody had to search for him, til they found him sleeping in the chicken coop. Charlotte's making sure there's no repeat of that. Sonny doesn't mind. He's face down on the ground, trying to build a cabin out of jimsonweed stalks.

"What're you going to name your kids?" she asks again.

"I'm not sure I'm having any."

"You better have names for them, just in case."

I can tell she's got hers figured out. "What are you?" I ask.

"Here's the girls . . ." She laces her hands behind her head and looks up at the sky as if they're written there. "The first is Tiffany Charlotte, after me. Then I'll have Melanie Crystal, Angelica Francine, and Heather Michele."

"Angelica Francine sounds stupid," Sonny mumbles."

"Shut up!" She pokes him with her foot, turns back to me. "What's all the names in your family?"

"There's me—Dawn Erica; Timothy O'Flynn and Elizabeth Kate. Mom's Eve Julia, and Dad's Douglas Everett Wesley."

"We have Shirley Ann and Bruce Philip Williams. Then there's Bruce Philip Jr.—that's Duke; Rufus Wade; James Harvey; Charlotte Annette; and Elmer Lynn."

"Who's Elmer Lynn?"

"Guess," Sonny mutters. Charlotte raises her eyebrows, nods toward him, looks back at me. "Does that give you some ideas?"

"I've got one for a boy."

"What?" She looks surprised.

I take a deep breath. "Camilo."

She stares. "That's what you called that duck, isn't it, Dawn? How do you say it again? Carmello?"

"No, Camilo. It's a Cuban name, from the island of Cuba."

"Sounds like a girl to me."

"It's not."

"Whose name is it?" She's staring harder.

"A baseball pitcher—the best in all the major leagues."

"What's he look like?"

"Tall, dark hair, dark eyes . . ." I close my eyes, picture him in my mind, open them again. Charlotte yips, "You got a crush on him."

"I don't, either; he's just—"

"Dawn, you're turning red."

"I'm not!"

"Girl, you are! Ain't she, Sonny?"

But Sonny doesn't even look up.

☼

Aunt Van's looking at my clothes. She says over the summer I've scattered them everywhere, and the half I didn't lose are ragged. She holds up a pair of jeans.

"Gracious, look how you've grown. These are the pants you were wearing when you came here, aren't they, Dawn? I remember the little flowers on the pocket."

"I hate those pants," I mutter. Nothing bores me more than clothes.

"I don't see why you won't let me take you into Lynville and get you something cute. All the girls are wearing pedal pushers now. I saw a pair printed with sailboats—you'd like that, wouldn't you?"

I don't want to hurt her feelings, but I think pedal pushers are stupid. "I might, but I'd want to see them first," I explain. Otherwise I'm afraid she'll buy them next time she's in town.

"And look at your sneakers—all torn up and dirty. At least we could get you a pair of Keds."

"I kind of like these Converse, 'cause they aren't pointy. Those pointy toes squish my feet."

She laughs and shakes her head. "When Ina and I were little, we went barefoot in summer. There was nothing we wanted more than a pair of pretty sandals. We would have crammed ourselves into them if we had to, and we probably would have had to, 'cause going barefoot made our feet spread. I have to buy wide shoes to this day."

I look at her feet. Her shoes *are* ugly—wide and black, with a little step-up heel and three holes for laces on each side. She sees me looking.

"I'm an old lady now, so I wear what's comfortable. But a pretty young girl like you, you can dress yourself up, know what I mean?"

"I guess I'm like you, Aunt Van. I just like comfortable stuff."

She sighs. "I wanted to get you something new for the day Doug and Evie come down. They haven't laid eyes on you for weeks. Don't you think they'd like to see you looking pretty?"

"Ummm . . . I'm not sure. But if you really want to get me something, a couple new pairs of jeans would be fine. They can be just like these." I turn around, show her the label that says *Wrangler.*

"But a little bigger." Aunt Van throws up her hands, like she's giving up. "All right, Dawn."

☼

Alec's new name is his strangest yet: Ramar. When he tells it, everybody gathers around and stares. "That don't sound American," Jimbo says.

"It's from India, I think. He got it off a TV show called *Ramar of the Jungle,* didn't you, Alec?"

He won't answer 'cause I called him by the wrong name. "Say it again," Charlotte says.

"Ramar—it's R-a-m-a-r."

"Why's he want to be called that?" Sonny asks.

"'Cause Ramar's an explorer. He rides on elephants and shoots at tigers. Once a rhino charged right at him, and he nearly died. Another time he got lost in the jungle and had to sleep all night up in a tree, so the cobras didn't get him."

"Staying in a tree too long is tough," Charlotte says.

"Ramar's not afraid. He's got a knife and a pistol both, and he can use 'em."

They look at Ramar: "Wow."

"He's got an assistant, too. His name is George."

"George," Sonny mutters. He and Ramar run off to the jimsonweeds to play.

☼

"Mama said you can spend the night, seeing as you're going home soon," Charlotte tells me later. "She says she'll make us a lemon-pudding cake, and we can play with paper dolls or listen to the radio til nine o'clock."

"Which night?" I ask.

"Tuesday or Wednesday. She has to check with Daddy though, to make sure it's okay."

"Where will we sleep?"

"In my room. I figure if you lay your head at one end of the bed, and me at the other, we'll be all right, long as we can keep from kicking each other."

"I never slept like that before." To me it doesn't sound real comfortable.

"You'll be the first girlfriend ever spent the night with me," Charlotte says. "It's going to be fun."

22

But Charlotte hasn't guessed what's coming—nobody has but Duke. He leaves a note behind him, under the pillow in the room he shares with Jimbo, Rufe, and Sonny. Since he sometimes leaves early to work at Tucker's, in the sheep pens, no one knows he's gone til suppertime. Then they run around calling; Charlotte even comes up to Moody and Van's and asks if we've seen him here. I run back with her. Turns out he wasn't at Tucker's all day, either, which puts Mr. Williams into a tailspin. Charlotte's mom thinks something might have happened to him. She's twisting her hands and crying. Then Sonny comes down from the bedroom:

"Y'all, look at this!"

"What?" Mr. Williams grabs the piece of paper. Something in his face makes me feel like hiding. When he's done reading, he rips it into little pieces.

"What?" Mrs. Williams is hanging on his arm, crying. "What is it, Bucky?"

"He's gone—gone for good, 'cause there ain't no way I'm taking him back."

"Gone where?" She's sobbing now.

"To the army. Says he already signed the papers; and he had to report this morning."

"Can they go and take him like that?"

"Sure they can—he's of age, ain't he?" He shakes her off his arm, pushes her away. She's crying, "Oh, my baby."

I want to leave, but I'm scared, 'cause Mr. Williams doesn't even know I'm here. But he's looking for someone else. He grabs Jimbo by the shoulder, pulls him close.

"Did you know?"

Jimbo's shaking like a wet dog. He starts crying before he even answers: "I didn't know nothing, Daddy, I swear."

His father slaps him hard across the face, once, twice. "You better tell me if you knew."

"I didn't know nothing."

He shoves him off and grabs for Rufe.

"What about you?"

"Nah, he didn't say nothing to me."

Mr. Williams shakes him by the shoulders. Rufe's

head rolls back and forth, back and forth. "You two was talking in the barn, I saw you there."

Rufe looks right at his father. A tiny glint comes in his eye. "He's gone now," he says.

Mr. Williams hits him with his fist, and Rufe goes down. Charlotte's mom scrambles on her knees to shield his face.

"Bucky, NO!"

He doesn't look at us, just heads for the door and slams it on his way outside.

⚹

Rufe's okay. Charlotte tells me the next morning when I'm in the barn with Star. "But Daddy's got an awful temper, doesn't he, Dawn?"

I don't say anything; I don't know what to say.

"Don't tell nobody, okay? If you tell, I'll get in trouble."

I keep quiet. Charlotte adds, "He's real sorry you seen him like that. If you come spend the night, it won't happen again."

"Oh."

"You're coming, aren't you, Dawn? I never had anybody come before."

"Probably." I don't want to say what I'm thinking, so I make up an excuse. "I just got to check with Van and Moody."

"That's good." Charlotte lies down in the straw, kisses Star's nose. "Ummmm," she says. "If I was rich, I'd have a velvet dress."

"What color?"

"Green." She's got her chin resting on her hands. "And I'd have gold shoes and a patent leather purse with a gold buckle."

"If I was rich . . ." I have to stop and think. "I'd have six ponies, and a swimming pool, and season tickets to the ball game. And I'd pay someone to stay in a laboratory day and night, until they found a cure for every disease in the whole world. All the sick people would be saved."

"Prayer saves," Charlotte says. She grins like she's teasing, puts her hands together. "You don't know anything about that, do you, Dawn? I bet you never said a prayer in your whole life."

She's still smiling, but her eyes are serious.

"I did," I say; but the truth is I can't remember whether I have or not.

"You can tell Jesus anything."

"Did you tell Him about Duke?"

"I told Him, but He knew already." She sighs. "He answered it was for the best. Told me Duke wasn't meant to spend his life inside them sheep pens."

"What about Rufe and Jimbo?"

"I didn't ask about them."

"Your dad shouldn't hit them like he did."

"That's not your business, Dawn."

"It is when I see it with my own eyes."

She gets mad. "You're not the judge of us."

I stand there staring at her. She glares back. She's getting redder and redder. Finally she says, "You know what we say about you?"

"What?" I don't really want to know. But that doesn't matter to Charlotte. Her words run together like bees swirling in a hive.

"You're a spoiled city girl that's never done a lick of work. You never even had a whipping. You waste your time daydreaming about being a baseball pitcher and other things that will never ever happen."

"That's not true!" I yell, but by then she's turned on her heel and flounced out the barn door.

23

Charlotte and I make up. We're in the barn. She claims she doesn't really think I'm spoiled; she said it 'cause last year she saw two girls fighting on the schoolbus, and one called the other "spoiled b——." She tells me the word. "Least I didn't say all that," she says.

"You better not."

"Better not what?"

"Call me a spoiled—" I'm not allowed to cuss. Charlotte starts giggling, and I do, too. "Say it," she says. "You have to say it."

"No, I don't."

"Yes, you do, Dawn. Say it."

"No!" I'm laughing out loud now. She tries to tickle me.

"You're afraid to say it, aren't you? You're afraid the boogeyman'll get you."

"Am not."

"Say it then."

"All right, I'll say it." I look around the barn to make sure no one else is here. Then I whisper in her ear.

After that we fall down on the straw and laugh so hard we cry.

☼

She still wants me to spend the night. She's bugging me about it: "You're coming, right, Dawn? You can come anytime on Tuesday."

I ask Uncle Moody at breakfast. He puts the newspaper down and stares at me with his dark eyes. "You think she asked her folks?"

"Yes, 'cause her mom said she's making us a special dessert."

He rubs his nose with the back of his hand, grunts, looks at Aunt Van. She looks back at him. She says, "You girls could stay up here."

I'm not sure why I hesitate. It's something about Charlotte saying: "I never had anyone come before," like so much is hanging on me saying yes.

"I guess I'll go," I say. "Charlotte wants to do it there, and I don't want to hurt her feelings."

"That's nice, Dawn." Aunt Van nods.

Uncle Moody says, "I'll leave the door unlocked. If you get homesick in the night, come home on the road—don't wander round the woods, like you did before."

"Okay."

He's watching me to see if I feel comfortable with what we've said. He puts on his cap, tugs on the brim, slurps the last swallow of coffee from his cup. He gets up like he's going to work. Then, out of the blue, he says, "I've been thinking about them kids."

Aunt Van's already got her mind on something else. "What kids?"

"Them kids down the road. Duke and Charlotte and all."

"What about them?"

"That boy run off and joined the army the first minute he could, you know, Van? And the army's not an easy life. . . ."

She's looking at him, trying to figure what he's getting at.

"What do you expect he was running from?" Uncle Moody asks, almost to himself.

"I don't know, Moody. Maybe he was sick and tired of working with those sheep."

"It could be that. But I've been thinking different."

"What?"

"I've been thinking maybe Bucky's a harsh master. Like that night Charlotte climbed the tree. She shouldn't have to do that."

"You know Evie would have done the same—or worse. She would have told the world we were *murderers*, if we'd said she couldn't go swimming."

"That's true . . ."

Aunt Van cuts her eyes toward me, then back, like maybe they shouldn't talk about grown-up stuff with me around. "If he's a little tough on them, I can see why. He works like a dog, and there's precious little to show for it: just bills, and that worn-out truck, and those kids clamoring for things he doesn't have."

Uncle Moody grunts.

"He's probably just worn out," Aunt Van says. She folds her arms. They remind me of thick white loaves of bread. "You know, Moody, instead of judging him, maybe we ought to judge ourselves. I bet there's more that we could do for them."

"Could be." He nods, his face serious. "We got extra, that's for sure."

"I bet they could use milk. Last I heard, their cow's near dry."

"I wouldn't begrudge them that." He looks at me. "You'd carry it over there, wouldn't you, Dawn?"

"Sure."

"And I got more tomatoes than any living soul could can, peaches and Seckel pears, too. Bucky has his pride, but if I say the produce's going to waste, I think he and Shirley will accept it."

"That's good." Uncle Moody tugs the brim of his cap again, looks out the window toward the truck. Aunt Van turns on the water in the sink. A cloud of steam rises around her. Out of the corner of my eye I think I see him pat her on the backside as he sidles past her, toward the door. She turns bright pink.

"Moody!"

"I'll be home for supper."

Red stands in the truckbed, wagging his tail, as the pickup heads down the driveway toward the road.

☼

Ramar's hurt we didn't ask him to the sleepover. We're at the planet, trying to explain about pajama parties: how they're a girl thing—embarrassing for me, since I don't really believe in that.

"Like we didn't ask could we sleep with you boys down under the oak tree that night," Charlotte says sweetly. "The night you wandered off looking for candy and claimed some ghosts scared you to death."

Ram looks mad.

"But that's not the point. The point is, we didn't ask to join your camp-out that night, did we? 'Cause the first thing y'all would have said is, we don't want no girls."

"*I* w-w-w-wouldn't."

"Maybe not you, Ram, but them others—you can bet on it."

He's not convinced. "W-w-w-why don't you sleep under the trees?" he asks. "Then all of us could come."

"That's the whole point." Charlotte's trying to be patient. "You think I want to spend the night with Sonny, Rufe, and Jimbo? I put up with them dummies every single day."

Ram's lower lip is sticking out. "It would be *fun*," he argues. Then, almost as an afterthought, he adds, "Being outside is better anyway."

He looks at me. I'm pretty sure he's worried about Charlotte's dad.

"What if it rains?" Charlotte grins. She thinks she's got him now.

"We could sleep down in Dawn's barn, with Star."

His stubbornness is puzzling her, then she thinks she has it figured out. "This is *my* party, Ram—not yours. If you want to plan one, go ahead, and then invite us, and we'll come." She turns toward me. "Right, Dawn?"

"I guess."

"What do you mean, I *guess*? I thought you were dying to come." She's starting to get mad.

"I am," I say weakly. I glance at Ram, then look away.

24

I go down to the Williamses' house at three o'clock. I take my toothbrush and pajamas and a book, because I usually read before I fall asleep.

You can see Charlotte's tried to clean her room. Clothes and pieces of paper are picked up off the hooked rug. For the first time ever the bed is made, with two pillows sitting at the head. "Ma gave me clean pillowcases." She shows me. "You can pick: flowers or stripes."

"I'll take . . . stripes." Charlotte throws it at me, then we throw the pillows back and forth, whacking each other. Feathers fly everywhere. Maybe this will be fun, after all.

But Sonny wants in on everything we do. Soon as he hears that pillow fight, he plunks himself down outside Charlotte's door and starts whining. It's low at first, so quiet that I have to ask: "What's that?"

Instead of answering she shoves open the door and hits him square in the middle of the back. He bellows like he's going to die. "Mama, Charlotte hit me! Waaaaah!"

Mrs. Williams hustles up the steps, but for once she's got Sonny dead to rights. "Hush that bawling, Sonny, you're just jealous. I'm making a lemon-pudding cake. Don't you want to lick the bowl?"

He scurries away. Charlotte and I lie on the bed and pretend she's her mom and I'm Sonny. "Hush, sweetie," she says smiling. "I'm making a poison sandwich just for you."

"Yum."

"How about a nice big bowl of pig snouts with sour-milk gravy?"

I lick my lips.

Then Charlotte asks, "What's the worst thing you ever ate?"

I don't even have to think about it. "Once, my mom took me to lunch at a French restaurant in Georgetown. She ordered something in French, and when it came she gave me a taste. You know what it was?"

"What?"

"It was CALF BRAINS!"

We both make gagging sounds. Charlotte asks, "Did you puke?"

"Almost. I had to drink six glasses of ginger ale to get the taste out of my mouth."

"Was your ma sorry?"

"No, she thought I was making a big fuss over nothing." We roll our eyes. "What's your worst?" I ask.

She takes her time. "Could be the night we was all sitting around eating spaghetti when Sonny tells us he dropped a handful of worms in the pot, too, on account of they look the same. Every single one of us got up from the table and went outside. I could hear Jimbo retching all the way across the yard."

"Oh, yuck!"

"Or it might have been the day Mama cooked fish eggs. She scraped them out of the belly of a mudcat and fried them up with bacon. Another time she and Daddy made a snapping turtle into soup. Its foot was floating in my bowl. You could see its little tiny claws."

"Ooooooooooh."

"I've had all kinds of awful stuff." Charlotte's proud of what she's been through. "Rufe likes to poke in the backwoods. He'll search out mushrooms, ramps, persimmons, and butternuts, too. Last spring he brung home greens so bitter they curled your stomach in a knot. And that ain't all: I've had wild-duck eggs and groundhog gravy and eel roasted on a stick."

"You didn't!"

"If you don't believe me, go ask!" She's grinning. "Daddy caught one in the river. Peeled the skin right off. Didn't taste that bad, to tell the truth."

"Eel!" I pretend to faint.

She nods. "I heard people eat snake, too. But you know the one thing I wouldn't eat, Dawn, no matter what they did to me?"

"What?"

"A big fat toad."

We both scream at the thought. "What if you were starving?" I ask Charlotte. We're laughing and rolling on the bed until one and then the other falls smack onto the floor. "I wouldn't," Charlotte keeps saying. I say, "Maybe you would."

☼

An hour later I'm sitting at the kitchen table with the rest of the Williams. Supper's porkchops, yams, applesauce, and homemade biscuits with jelly. Charlotte's dad says grace. Tonight he's quiet, not like the other times I've seen him; and I see his face is lined from working in the sun and wind. He folds his hands and asks a blessing on the meal, his family, and mine, too. He prays that Mom gets well enough to walk again. His voice is calm and soothing. Behind closed eyes I picture Mom and Dad, Timmy and Beth, like they're near enough to touch.

After that there's mostly chewing sounds, then swallowing, with now and then somebody saying, "Pass the milk." Finally Jimbo asks, "How's Star?"

"Getting better—the vet's been giving her shots. Uncle Moody thinks they've done her good. . . ."

"She gonna live?" Jimbo asks.

"We still don't know for sure."

"Everybody's time comes," Mr. Williams says quietly.

After that's the lemon-pudding cake. We all get seconds, til there's nothing on that platter but a smear of lemon sauce. Mrs. Williams asks if I drink coffee. I say, "No, ma'am;" but Rufe and Charlotte have a half cup each, with canned milk and lots of sugar. Then we go outside for hide-and-seek.

It's a good time all around. Sonny's *it:* we all beat him to home base, so he's *it* again, til finally Rufe takes pity and says that he'll be *it* a while. But Rufe's good; no matter where we hide we hear him creeping past; and the sounds of our breathing get his attention. It's like he has a second sense about hiding.

"One-two-three on Dawn!"

I scramble for home, but he beats me, and I'm *it.*

☼

We go to bed at nine, while it's still light. Charlotte's window looks out on the branches of a tree. We talk softly, then while she falls asleep I watch the light grow dim and the solid darkness of the tree fade into night. At Uncle Moody's, I'd be listening to the ball game now. I pretend I'm hearing it: "Pascual rears back and throws—it's a breaking ball. Strike Two! Nellie Fox backs out of the box and scuffs the dirt. He really wants to get this hit, but the pitcher's staring, and the next ball breaks across the plate. . . ." Sleep comes, then, and I waft into the pillow, thinking, *Stripes, I choose stripes. . . .*

25

It isn't morning when I wake up. The tree is barely visible in the dark frame of the window; and stars sprinkle the sky like specks of salt. From the far side of the bedroom wall there is a sound. It comes again, a low harsh whisper, and an answer back. I can't hear what they're saying, but I know the voices: Charlotte's folks. I adjust my pillow, lie back, and close my eyes.

But the sounds don't go away, and slowly the room comes into focus. Charlotte's head is a lump at the far end of the bed; her breathing's soft and regular, marking seconds in the night. A whisper comes again, low and urgent: "No!"

There's more then, back and forth. My heart thumps in my chest, 'cause I'm afraid. What if Mr. Williams starts to hit his wife? Will I just lie here listening? I toss and turn, then I decide that I'll get up. I slide my sneakers on, slip a shirt over my pajama top. The hallway to the stairs runs the opposite direction from their bedroom. I put one hand on the wall and feel my way to the first step down.

After that it's one foot, then another, til I reach the bottom of the stairs. There's a light shining dimly from the kitchen, where the screen door leads outside. Maybe they leave that on, in case you're going to the outhouse. But when I tiptoe in, there's Rufe, sitting by himself at the kitchen table. He's surprised to see me. "Hey, Dawn," he says softly. Then he asks, "Did they wake you?"

"I guess."

"It's no big thing," he says. "When he gets mad, he shouts."

I don't say anything.

"Do your folks argue?"

"Sometimes. But I don't usually hear them, 'cause their bedroom's on the other side of the apartment."

"Let's go outside," he says. "I'll take you for a ride."

✧

The night air's soft and warm. Crickets are chirping even though it's late. Rufe says that's 'cause it rained the other day. He opens the passenger-side door of an old Buick, then settles himself into the driver's seat.

"Where to?"

I'm feeling shy, so no place comes to mind. A half moon's shimmering over the barn. Rufe points: "How about up there?"

"Okay."

"Prepare for takeoff."

"Ready."

"Five—four—three—two—one!"

A breeze stirs through the open window. For some reason it feels like we're angling upward, into air. Rufe's face is touched by moonlight; I can see his freckles. Tufts of hair spill over his ears. He's grinning now. "Don't this feel good, Dawn? We're on our way, and nobody can stop us."

"I want to be the moon's best pitcher," I tell him. He laughs and says, "At least you'll be the first."

He's pretending to drive, turning the wheel this way and that. He fiddles with the knob of the radio. "What kind of music do you like?"

"I don't know." Truth is, most of what I listen to is baseball.

"How 'bout this?" His voice is sweet and low. He sings a song that Van likes, too: "Whenever I want you, all I have to do is Dre-e-e-e-eam, dream, dream, dream."

I'm feeling shy. He turns and looks at me. "You ain't scared, are you?" he asks.

"No."

"You know I got a girlfriend, right?"

I nod. He shows me her picture. It's wrinkled and dog-eared from being in his pocket. I can barely make out the woman's face, but she looks old.

"What's her name again?"

"Lois." He says it softly. "She helped me out, when I was in the hospital," he adds. "When I was hurting, she used to come and rub my back—she was my nurse, see? Then we would talk." He turns toward me. "She told me I could call her girlfriend if I want; but she's got someone else. But I don't mind. The way her hands felt on my back, I never felt anything that good before. Before I left I asked her would she kiss me, and she did. You know how good that felt, Dawn? You ever been kissed like that?"

"No . . ."

"I'll show you what it's like."

He leans over then, presses his lips to mine. I taste something warm and sweet, like fresh-cut hay. He pulls back, smiling.

"Nice, ain't it?"

I nod, but I'm too shy to ask him to do it again.

26

When we go back inside, the house is still. I sneak upstairs and into Charlotte's bed. I'm exhausted, but something's stirring inside me, something strange and new. I remember Mom saying: "You're so serious, Dawn. Don't you ever just feel like dancing?" Back then, I didn't know what she meant, but now I lie here, hugging my pillow, whispering, "Yes."

☼

Charlotte doesn't wake up as early as me. I stay still a while, watching her sleep; then I get up, put on my clothes, and run to the barn to practice pitching. I rub Star's head and feed her oats before I get my glove and ball.

I pitch better than ever: my curve is breaking the way I like it, only wider; and the fast ball zings. Maybe it's because I had to rest when Star was sick.

When I've done a hundred, I run back down to Charlotte's. Mrs. Williams is in the kitchen, frying bacon. She looks surprised when I open the screen door.

"You been out already, Dawn?"

"I had to check on Star."

"Was Moody down there?"

"Not yet."

She shakes her head. "I sure appreciate that milk y'all brought down. Moody and Van are good neighbors, even where our ideas are different. I hope some day we'll have extra to give them." She talks on nervously, more to herself than to me. The bacon sizzles, and I smell something like biscuits in the oven. She opens the side door of the range, checks on the fire, then adds a stick of wood. Sonny bursts into the room like a jack-in-the-box.

"Dawn! Did you stay all night? Did you sleep with Charlotte? Did you see the baby ring snakes I put under the bed?"

"You did not," Mrs. Williams says; but Sonny's nodding his head up and down:

"I did! I wanted Dawn to see them, 'cause they're wiggly!"

At almost the same second there's a screech from upstairs: "Ma, come quick!"

"Charlotte's 'feard of snakes," Sonny tells me.

"Ma!"

"I'll go," I say to Mrs. Williams, and she smiles her thanks.

☼

Charlotte's standing on her bed. There's a snake about three inches long on her hooked rug; it's black, with a little orange band around its neck. I've seen these before, in the cracks of the cement foundation of Uncle Moody's porch, and I know they don't bite. I pick it up and put it in my pocket.

Charlotte's staring at me. "Dawn," she says, "what happened to your hair?"

"What do you mean?"

She's looking intently now; the snake is forgotten.

"It's different."

"I combed it." I turn red.

"You never did before!"

"That's 'cause I didn't want to!"

She keeps staring at me. "Where'd you get the comb?" she asks finally.

"There's one down in the barn, hanging on a nail."

"You been to the barn already? How come you didn't wake me?"

"I wanted to pitch."

She looks pained. "When you sleep over, you're supposed to stay til the other person wakes up. You don't just go running off."

"I'm here now."

She grins suddenly, showing I'm forgiven. "And Mama's making bacon! Let's run, before the boys eat every bit!"

☼

But the only ones at breakfast are Jimbo, Charlotte, Sonny, Mrs. Williams, and me. It turns out Mr. Williams had to leave at five to do the Tucker's milking, and Rufe's in the barn squeezing the last few drops out of their cow, Doll. Jimbo says grace, 'cause he's the oldest male. We have bacon, biscuits, and wild honey. Mrs. Williams says she'll make eggs, too, if anybody wants them; but we say no. "Wonder what Duke's eating," Sonny says. "Wonder if he's got a helmet and a pair of boots."

"Shush," Jimbo says. "Don't start."

"It's all right, Jimmy," Mrs. Williams says. "We all wonder how he is."

"Not Daddy," Sonny says. "He said good riddance."

"He don't mean it—it's just Duke hurt his feelings, running off."

"Did he hurt your feelings, Ma?" Sonny asks.

"Hush, Sonny." She turns her head, but her eyes are filled with tears.

I hang around at the table, waiting for Rufe to come; when he doesn't, I help Mrs. Williams clear and scrape the dishes. She looks surprised, and pleased. "Thank you, Dawn."

"Thanks for letting me come. That lemon-pudding cake was very good."

"I'll make you another one, next time you're at Van and Moody's. You'll come at Thanksgiving, won't you?"

"I'm not sure about Thanksgiving—we might go to my dad's parents in Pennsylvania—but we'll be here for Christmas."

"At Christmas, then." She smiles. "Eve should be walking good by then."

"I hope."

"I hope so, too, honey." She pats me on the arm before I go outside.

✦

I never do see Rufe that day. Charlotte and I go down to Ram's and play with him. Now that the summer's nearly over, Auntie Merle's used to us: when she sees us coming over the hill, her screechy voice calls "Delbert!" until he pokes his head out of the toolshed: "I'm here!" He gestures for us to look at something.

He's got a little wire strung from a hook on the door to a peg sunk in the dirt. When he opens the door the wire gets taut. Then he can pluck it with one hand. He goes up and down the wire, making tones like a scale. "Play something," Charlotte says. He picks out "My Country 'Tis of Thee." She tries it, then, but it isn't as easy as it looks.

"He can play the piano, too," I tell her.

"How do you know?"

"Uhhhh . . . sometimes he's with me when I practice. I found out he can play almost as good as me."

"I want to see," Charlotte says.

We troop up to the house. Aunt Van is in the kitchen, peeling Seckel pears. She smiles when she sees us at the door: "How was last night, girls?" Then she sees my hair. "My, *that* looks nice. Did Charlotte fix it for you?"

"No, I did it myself." I wish people wouldn't talk about the way I look.

Aunt Van goes on: "I'm running out to Paula Tucker's. She wants my recipe for ginger beef, 'cause Walter's two brothers are coming up on Monday, and she wants to make them something special." She gives us a long look—more Charlotte and me than Ram. "Can I trust y'all to be good for a half hour, while I'm gone?"

"We'll be *real* good," Charlotte says.

We practice the piano soon as she goes out. Charlotte pulls a chair beside the bench and watches everything. I start by playing a scale, then Ram plays it, too. After a few more scales I play "Home on the Range." Then Ram plays it. We do the same with "Take Me out to the Ball Game" and "America the Beautiful." After that Charlotte holds up her hand like a traffic cop. "You can stop now, Dawn," she says.

"How come?"

"Compared to Ram's, your playing is"—she stops, searching for the word—"horrendous."

"It is NOT!" What kind of friend is Charlotte, anyway? I turn my back on her and stomp upstairs.

I go into the bathroom, to be alone and think. My angry face stares from the mirror. I notice that the way I combed my hair down in the barn makes it slant across my forehead, giving me a one-eyed look. I take Aunt Van's comb and even the part, swish the hair back on both sides, then pull it forward and mess it up, so no one can tell I fooled with it.

When I go back down, they're lying outside on the glider. They're giggling with each other; then when I show up Charlotte says, "You did something *else* to your hair!"

"Did not!"

"Did! Can't you see, Ram? Can't you see she did?"

He stares like he never saw my hair before, like maybe he never noticed I *had* hair.

"My sister has pink curlers. She was going to w-w-w-wear them to school, but Mom said n-n-no."

I ask what school. Ram and his sister go to Franklin, which is near my friend Ellen's house. I tell him that.

"She's in fifth grade—she's got dark hair, and she gets in trouble 'cause she can't keep still. She has a little brother named Mike."

Charlotte assumes Ellen is white. "They got white and colored kids in the same school?"

"Yeah, it changed when I was in first grade."

She shakes her head like she never heard of that. Later, though, she seems subdued. "Y'all probably going to get to see each other when you go back. I'll be down here by my lonesome."

"You got Sonny and Jimbo and Rufe."

Charlotte doesn't bother to answer.

"And you got the kids in your class. They're nice, aren't they?"

"They're all right." She's looking straight ahead. "Only they make fun of us, 'cause we ain't got TV, and they get their clothes from Penney's, and we don't. They wear nylons to school, too. Daddy says I can't have stockings til I turn fifteen."

"I don't want them," I say. "Mom says they're hot and sticky, and they get runs if you brush against something. Then you have to buy new ones."

"Fay Early got six pair for her birthday. When she bends over you can see her garter belt. She's even got a girdle."

"W-w-w-what's that?" Ram asks.

"It's a rubber thing you wear, like underwear, except it's tight."

He thinks we're making it up. "Rubber underwear?"

We nod.

"And that's not all about the girls at school," Charlotte says. "You know what else? They got one thing on their mind, and one thing only."

"What's that?" I ask.

"It's boys. All they think about is boys."

27

That night my mom calls. She's feeling way better, and she can walk with crutches now. "It took a while to get used to them, but now when I go up and down the hallways, I practically fly."

I imagine her like some crazy dark-haired angel, sailing around the hospital. That makes me laugh.

"And Monday I'll try walking with a metal cane. That's probably what I'll have when we come for you."

"When's that?"

"Next Saturday—about a week from now. The summer's flown past, hasn't it?"

I don't answer. Some parts have been fast, others—the worrying parts—seemed to last forever.

"Are you looking forward to coming home? Or have they turned you into a farm girl?"

"A little of both, I guess."

"What have you and Charlotte been up to?"

"Nothing really." I tell about spending the night down there, leaving out the scene with Rufe.

"I remember Shirley Williams from when we were small—her family name was Parker. Now and then we used to play together. She was such a kind girl— she looked after the kindergarten kids, and held their hands if they were scared. Later, sometimes, they'd be embarrassed, and they'd make fun of her. Even though she was older, she didn't seem to know how to fight back, or stand up to them. I don't think she had a mean bone in her whole body."

"Did you stick up for her?"

Mom sounds sad. "Most of the time we brushed her off as if she wasn't even there. The Parkers were quiet people; and the rest of us were caught up in our own world—ponies and clothes and soft-ball. . . ."

"Did you know her when she married Bucky?"

"No, by then we'd gone our separate ways. I didn't even know she *had* married til Van told me they'd moved into that old house. By then she had a bunch of kids, and I had you and Timmy, too."

"Maybe you could be friends, like Charlotte and me."

She laughs. "We live in different worlds, Dawn."

"That doesn't mean you can't be friends."

She gets serious now, maybe she can hear from my voice that something's bothering me. "Why do you want us to be friends?" she asks.

"Because I think she might be lonely. . . ."

"Oh, Dawn . . ." her voice catches. "Did you tell Van? She would visit her, I know."

I don't say anything.

"Talk to her, sweetie. She's so busy, she probably doesn't think about Shirley. But if she had any idea of that, she would."

"Okay."

"I'll see you soon, all right? I love you."

"I love you, too." That's the last thing we say before the phone clicks off.

☼

But I don't want to talk to Van. I tried talking to her about Mr. Williams, and it didn't work. Not only that, but I feel guilty 'cause of the piano trick. Later, at Planet Kid, I tell Charlotte and Sonny.

"Aunt Van's telling everyone how I've improved. That's 'cause whenever Ram plays, she thinks it's me!"

Charlotte understands the problem. "Preacher warned us about lying. He said you get tangled in your own deceit, twisting and turning like a fly in a spider's web."

I don't like the picture she's painting. "I didn't lie," I protest. "I never said it was me, or it wasn't. She just concluded that it was, because she didn't look."

She eyes me sternly. "You could have said, 'That wasn't me, Aunt Van.' "

"Yeah, I could have." I feel miserable.

"Preacher told us liars burn in hell." Sonny's sprawled on the ground, scratching all over like he's got fleas. Charlotte pokes him: "Cut it out."

"I don't believe in hell."

They both turn. "What did you say?" Sonny asks.

I repeat it. Their mouths are open. Charlotte asks, "What do you believe in, then?"

"I don't know."

"You ought to come to Sunday school with us. They'll tell you about hell, and the devil, too. They even got pictures someone took down there." Sonny's stopped scratching.

"What's it like?"

"It's dark and smoky, and the people ain't got clothes. They're hollering, 'cause the devil's sticking fire on their toes, and they can't get nothing to eat."

"How do you know the pictures are real?"

He opens his mouth to answer, then instead he starts scratching his stomach.

Charlotte grabs his arm: "You're driving me crazy."

"Let go!"

"Then cut it out!" She smacks him one, and he starts crying. She yells, "What in the world is wrong with you?"

He lifts his shirt. His stomach's covered with red spots. We stare at them.

"You've got the chicken pox," I say. "I know, 'cause Timmy had them last year."

We crowd around and look. There're a couple on his forehead and his chin. "Yuck," Charlotte says. "We better take him home."

Sonny keeps crying. He's working up a head of steam: "I want 'em off!"

"They don't come off."

"You mean they're here for good?"

"They'll disappear in a couple weeks," I tell him; but by now he's bellowing so loud he doesn't even hear.

☼

We run into Rufe on their front porch. It's the first time I've seen him since the other night. My face gets red but I can't help smiling. He smiles back. He doesn't even notice I'm embarrassed.

"How you doing, Dawn?"

"I'm okay, but Sonny's got chicken pox."

"Daaaag." Sonny's bawling like a bull calf. Rufe squats down and looks him over.

"Get rid of 'em, okay, Rufe? I don't want 'em on my skin."

"I'll get rid of 'em." He nods.

"How can you get rid of chicken pox?" I'm staring at him now.

"Easy." He holds one hand over Sonny's head, passes the other up and down like it's a ray gun shooting magic rays. "That ought to do it."

"You cured me of the chicken pox?"

"Sure did."

Sonny looks confused, but at least he's stopped blubbering. "But I still got 'em. Look here, Rufe . . ."

Rufe looks carefully, nods. "Looks like 'em, all right, but it ain't the same. These here is false chicken pox. In a couple weeks, they'll peel right off."

"You sure?" Sonny looks doubtful.

"Course, I'm sure."

"I won't have nary a one?"

"Nary a single one."

28

In the meantime, Sonny's got the chicken pox real bad. Charlotte says he was up all last night, crying and moaning. This morning Mrs. Williams looks tired. Her shoulders are slumped, and she hardly turns her head when Charlotte asks her, "Mama, are we out of milk?"

Her voice is vague. "I asked Rufe if Doll gave any, but he didn't answer."

Charlotte looks at me, rolls her eyes. When we go into the next room she whispers, "She and Daddy had a fight last night."

"How come?"

"Daddy wanted Sonny quiet, so he could sleep, because he had to be to work at four. But Mama couldn't get Sonny settled down."

"What happened?"

"She heated whiskey and put it in a glass of milk, but he couldn't drink it—he's got the spots inside his throat. He just kept bawling and carrying on. Then Daddy hollered if he didn't shut up, he'd give Sonny something real to cry about. Finally Rufe took him to the barn to sleep. He and Duke made a hideout there."

"Can I see it?"

She shakes her head. "It's not for playing. And it's secret, Dawn—top secret."

-☼-

She and Ram figure out how I feel about Rufe. We're at the planet, talking about who's good on TV. Charlotte says, "Captain Midnight is the best." Ram says Roy Rogers, or—second choice—the Lone Ranger. I think about Camilo Pascual, but he's not really a TV star 'cause he's only on when the ball games are broadcast, which is rare. They talk about the show called *Mickey Mouse Club*. Charlotte's seen it once, over at Fay Early's. It's got a set of twins who can sing and dance. Fay saw their picture in a magazine and cut it out. Charlotte says they're cute, with blue eyes and red hair.

"I like red hair," I say.

Charlotte says, "My kids will all be blond."

"How do you know?"

"Because I do."

"But they could look like their father."

"My kids won't have a daddy. It's going to be all me."

We start laughing then. Ram looks confused. I can tell nobody's told him certain stuff, 'cause he's just nine years old.

"My kids may have dark hair," I say. "Or maybe orangey-tan."

"Orangey-tan?"

I nod. "You know—like Rufe's."

They're looking at me now. I turn bright red. They can't help but notice. "You're blushing," Charlotte says. "How come you're blushing, Dawn?"

"I'm not." I put my hands over my cheeks, to cover them.

"Is it something about Rufe?"

"No."

But they still think it is. Charlotte's looking at me funny. "What *is* it, Dawn?" She's squinting now, like she can't believe her eyes. "You care for him?"

"Unh-unh."

"How come you're red, then?"

"I'm not."

"You are." She tries to pull my hands away. We're staring at each other. If I say yes, I'm afraid that she will laugh out loud. Instead she says, "Of all the people you could like, you picked my brother?"

I give a little nod. She keeps on staring for a minute. Then we both start giggling.

"I can't believe it," she says. "Dawn and Rufe . . ."

☼

They tell him right away. Next time I see him, down by the Williamses' shed, he's grinning all over. Jimbo's grinning, too. Jimbo's got his hands on his hips. "There she is, Rufe—look at her, standing there. She's nice-looking, for a girl."

"Sure she is," Rufe says.

"A girl?"

"No, Jimmy—good-looking. I *know* she's a girl."

"She can throw, too. Almost tore my hand up, pitching so hard."

Rufe nods. I see a faint flush under his freckles.

"She's going to the majors," Jimbo says. "She might be famous. If we get TV, we can turn it on and see her there."

"Maybe so."

"Hey, Dawn!" Sonny's leaning out the upstairs window. He's got about a thousand spots all over his face. "You want to play with me? We can play Chutes and Ladders. I got all the pieces but one."

I don't really want to; I want to stay right where I am, but it's so embarrassing that I nod and go inside.

☼

Sonny shares a room with his two brothers. Duke's bed is gone now; where it used to be there's just a rectangle of space. But the bedroom is full of cardboard boxes stuffed with clothes and mismatched boots. The walls are lined with newspaper, to keep out the cold. I see baseball scores from 1951, old classifieds, ads from A&P and Acme. "Do you read these?" I ask Sonny.

"Duke used to, sometimes," he answers. "He's the only one of us could really read."

"What about Rufe?"

"They put him back in seventh grade again. He says if he don't learn nothing this year, he's getting out." Sonny's setting up the game. "Jimbo don't like school, neither, but I do. I like to play dodge. I can dodge so good, one time I was the last one out."

☼

We play a couple games of Chutes and Ladders. I let Sonny win, 'cause he's sick. Each time he's pleased as punch.

"I'm better than you," he says finally. "But I won't tell no one."

Then I remember something. "Where are those photographs?" I ask.

"What photographs?"

"The ones of hell."

"Oh." He's not nervous, so I don't think he made it up. "They're at Sunday school, inside a book."

"Can you bring it home? I really want to see them."

He seems doubtful. "I'll ask my teacher," he says. "But I don't think you can."

"How come?"

"You don't know, Dawn?"

"Know what?"

He looks at me sadly. "You're not like us," he says.

"What do you mean?"

"You ain't saved."

It takes me a minute to understand. "You mean 'cause I don't go to church, Sonny?"

He nods. "Charlotte and me play with you anyway, because you're nice."

"You make it sound like you're special, and I'm not."

"It ain't your fault, Dawn. One day you'll wake up and know the truth."

29

Ram's folks are coming this Saturday, same as mine. Auntie Merle's making a ham and a turkey for supper that night. Ram says she cleaned her little house from top to bottom. Now when he goes inside he has to leave his shoes on the front steps, so he doesn't track in dirt.

Aunt Van's cleaning, too. We still practice the piano every day. I've been trying to pick a time when she'll come in the living room and see us there, so she'll understand that Ram's the good one. But she always seems to be vacuuming, or beating the rugs, or watering the flowers out front. I even tell her, "Ram's learning the piano. Would you like to hear him play?"

"You mean Delbert?"

"Yeah, we call him Ram."

"Didn't you call him something else before?"

"We used to call him Alec. . . ."

"Alec? I thought it was Willie."

"We only called him Willie for a little while. That came after Roy."

Aunt Van looks dazed. "Why don't you call him by his real name?" she asks.

"Because he doesn't like it."

"Maybe he's got a middle name you could use."

"I never thought of that."

But the upshot is she doesn't hear him play. I start to think that if she's going to, I'll have to plan it in advance.

※

Charlotte's upset I'm going home. "You're my best friend," she tells me while we're lying on our burlap pillow bags at Planet Kid. "You're the first one ever spent the night at my house. And you know stuff about me no one else does."

"About your dad, you mean?"

She nods. We sit there for a while. "You should tell me something about you," she says.

"Like what?"

"A secret. Something you never told anybody."

Everyone knows I want to be a pitcher. It takes me a while to think of something else. When I do, my cheeks burn, 'cause I'm ashamed:

"One day, when Mom was sick, I took Timmy to the park. He was swinging, and a little girl ran up to him. His swing must have hit her in the head and knocked her down. She screamed, and her mom ran over and started screaming, too, 'cause the girl was bleeding a lot. The woman yelled at Timmy, 'Where's your mother?' I was sitting behind the slide with a book, so he couldn't see me; but I saw everything. He pointed up the street, toward our building, but he was crying so hard no words came out. He tried to call me, I could hear him trying to say, 'Dawn, Dawn'; but I stayed where I was. I didn't want the woman to yell at me."

"It sounds like it wasn't even his fault," Charlotte says.

"No, the mother was just so upset. She shouldn't have screamed at Timmy like that. But I should have gone to help him."

"You never told anyone?"

I shake my head. "Just you."

"Next time, it'll be different, Dawn. Next time, when he calls you, you'll go."

"I hope so."

☼

The next day at breakfast, I ask if Charlotte can spend the night. Aunt Van hesitates; maybe she's thinking of all the cleanup she's already done. Then she says yes.

"As long as it's okay with Charlotte's mom and dad."

"Can she come tonight?"

"I don't see why not. I might even have time to make you girls egg custard."

"Hooray!"

I run tell Charlotte.

❖

She's in their garden, pulling weeds. She looks tired, though it isn't even nine o'clock. Her mom's sitting on their junky porch with Sonny in her lap. She sees me before Charlotte does.

"Hey, Mrs. Williams."

"Hello, Dawn."

"How's Sonny doing?"

"Poor little thing, he's plastered with baking soda, but the blisters smart anyway. Then he scratches, and turns himself into a bloody mess." She sighs. "Bucky's a light sleeper, so Sonny's whimpering keeps him awake. Then he gets ornery, too." Charlotte's mom laughs suddenly, but it doesn't sound like a real laugh—the sound is dry, like coughing. "It'll all be over soon," she says. "Chicken pox just lasts a week or so."

"When my brother had it, the doctor gave him special medicine to stop the itch. I think it made him sleepy, too."

She nods. "We don't have money for that, hon. Without Duke's pay, we're just scraping to get by." She's looking off, over the fencerow, as if she's watching something there. Then she turns back toward me, shakes her head. "Don't listen to me, Dawn. You kids should be out playing, having fun."

"That's okay." I feel bad now. "If I can help you, let me know."

☼

Charlotte's been working all this time. I go over where she is, tell her about the invitation. She isn't as excited as I thought. "Help me with these weeds," she mutters. "Then we'll talk."

Pulling weeds is hard. When you get a big one by the roots, it comes up suddenly and sprays dirt right in your face. Before long I'm coated with a layer of dust and sweat. Then Charlotte says, "We're done." We pull a bucket of water from the well, dump half on her and half on me. Then we sit down under a bush to rest.

"I thought you'd want to come," I say. "Aunt Van's going to make egg custard. That's your favorite, isn't it?"

She nods. "Nobody makes custard better than your aunt Van."

"What is it, then?"

She sits for a minute. Her hair is streaming where the water splashed. With it straight and limp like that, she looks a little like her mom. "I'm worried," she says finally.

"What about?"

"Since Sonny got sick, he's been fussing every night. Daddy's upset, too. He says his nerves are shot, 'cause he can't sleep. I'm afraid something bad could happen."

We're just sitting there like we have a thousand times this summer, when I see Charlotte's leg sticking out from under her blue skirt. The skin is pale and spotted with dirt, from weeding, and I notice suddenly that her bones are smaller than mine, more delicate. It would be easy for someone to snap those bones. I get scared then.

"You've got to come," I wheedle. "I came to your house, when you asked."

"That was different. You didn't have a reason to stay home."

"But it's wrong for you to hurt my feelings."

She doesn't look at me.

"Anyway, you're probably overreacting." My folks say this to me, when I'm upset. I add to my argument. "I remember how worried I was, when Mom had her operation. Your imagination goes crazy, thinking of what could be . . ." I look her in the eyes, swallow, plunge on: "I bet you nothing bad will happen at all."

30

Charlotte spends the night anyway. As soon as her mom hears she's invited, she says, "Charlotte, go. I'll feel better if you're having a good time."

"What about you, Ma?"

"Don't worry so much, sweetie. Everything will be okay."

Sonny's not so sure. "I want to go with Dawn. I should get to go, because I'm sick."

"That's the reason you *can't* go," Mrs. Williams says patiently. "You can't give everyone the chicken pox."

"No fair!" Sonny's whining.

"Let's you and me go down behind the barn and pick some blackberries. Then I'll make us a cobbler."

He stops crying then. His mom picks up a dented metal pail that's lying on the porch, and the two of them head off.

Charlotte, Ram, and I are at the planet. We're bored, 'cause we've played every game we know a million times over the summer. Then Ram says, "Let's play soldiers."

Charlotte's doubtful. "That's a boy game, Ram."

"My sister plays."

Charlotte and I exchange looks. Ram's sister, Carrie, is older than us, and in eighth grade. But maybe he's just lying, to get what he wants.

"How do you play it?" Charlotte asks.

"I'm the general, you're the sergeant, and Dawn's the private."

Maybe 'cause we're bored, Charlotte and I agree to give it a try.

At first I think soldiers is a really stupid game. We march around singing war songs and waving make-believe flags. Charlotte's in front of me, 'cause she's higher rank. I don't go to the conference in the officers' tent; I have to wait outside, to hear my orders. Which are to charge into a battle where my unit's outnumbered fifty to one. I kill a lot of them on my way out. Then I writhe and twist, 'cause of all the wounds I've got. General Ram gives a speech over my dead body. "He w-w-was the jewel of the regiment. . . ."

"She," I hiss.

"Shut up," he whispers back.

The game picks up when Rufe and Jimbo come. They've played soldiers before, and they like it. Rufe doesn't mind that he's fourteen, which seems old for this game, and he also doesn't mind being a private, like me. We huddle beside the fake campfire while the officers have another conference. We pretend we're cooking bacon and potatoes. "There's nothing in the world as good as bacon," he tells me.

"You should try Aunt Van's egg custard. When I get home from this war, that's the first thing I'm going to eat."

He leans back on his elbows, stretches his long legs.

"This little campfire don't do a soldier too much good," he says.

I ask him if he's killed anyone.

"Two or three dozen, I reckon, all in the line of duty."

"Did you get wounded?"

"Sure did. Got my leg halfway torn up. The medics thought they'd have to cut it off, but then they changed their minds."

"It's a wonder that you're here in camp, with an injury like that."

"Oh, it ain't as bad as I made it out to be." He slides his pant leg up and flexes his muscle. The calf of his leg is a mass of freckles and red hair.

Charlotte, Ram, and Jimbo come from the tent, which is just a sheet spread over some jimsonweeds. Ram salutes. We salute back. Lt. Jimbo tells us our orders.

"Company A, there's a good chance you'll die in enemy hands. But if you do, we'll give y'all a medal."

"We won't, either. You ain't sending us to die like you did Dawn."

The officers confer. General Ram announces he will lead the charge himself.

"Whoooeee." Rufe's impressed. We march around from place to place, stopping at the barn to pat Star. She switches her ears forward like she's glad to see us, rubs her head against our hands. Then we march out. Ram lines us up in front of the barn, turns around, yells, "Charge!"

Tut-tut-tut-tut-tut!! I can't remember, later, who makes these sounds, or which of us dies first. We're writhing on the ground, moaning and weeping. Charlotte's still not hit. Then she falls, too, clutching her chest. Jimbo's crawling along, dragging his legs behind him. "I'm living, but I'm crippled for life," he says.

"Tell the others about us, okay, pal? Tell them we fell on the glory field."

"All right."

"Tell them General Ram led his soldiers into heaven, like a troop of angels." Charlotte's eyes stay closed but her voice is strong.

"Tell them Aunt Van finished the custard, and it's on the front porch, waiting to be served."

We open our eyes. Van's standing by the fence, looking puzzled.

"Whoooeee," Rufe says. "That sounds better than being dead."

☼

Uncle Moody sets the cot up in my room, and Aunt Van brings a pillow and clean sheets. Charlotte's looking through my baseball stuff. "These cards are the same players, Dawn . . . Why do you need more than one?"

"Some are rookie cards, like that Pete Ramos—that's valuable now, 'cause he's famous, but he wasn't when he started out."

"How much is it worth?"

"Two dollars. But Mr. Hooper says in ten years, it could be twenty. And my autographed ball is worth even more." I'm nervous when she handles my cards. I try to keep them in perfect shape.

"How long have you collected baseball cards?"

"Since I was eight."

"That's a long time." But she's not really interested in them. She pokes through my dresser drawers, pulling out books and clothes.

"Look at this, Dawn. I never even saw you wearing it." She's fingering a flowered blouse Aunt Margie sent me for my birthday. Then she holds up a pair of pants. "These are nice."

"I don't like green."

"I do." She tries them on, but they sag around her waist. She pulls the flowered shirt over her head. The pink flowers in the fabric bring out the color in her cheeks.

"That looks great on you."

She stares into the mirror, hugs herself across the chest. "It's so pretty, Dawn."

"You can have it."

"Are you sure?"

"I'm sure."

She turns and hugs me quick.

✧

We don't fall asleep until midnight, 'cause we stay up giggling and telling scary stories. Charlotte claims she saw a ghost one night when they were driving home from Lynville.

"How close were you?"

183

"As far as to that wall."

I feel a shiver up my spine. It's thrilling and scary both at once. "How did you get so close?"

"See, we were coming home from church. Sonny was asleep on Mama's lap, but the rest of us kids was in the back of the truck. Mama had put some blankets there, to keep us warm. Jimbo and Rufe covered themselves up and went to sleep—that's one thing you should know about Rufe, Dawn—he can sleep through anything. Anyway, it was just Duke and me, sitting there, with our backs leaned up against the cab. He was looking one way and I was looking t'other. All of a sudden I seen something moving. I poked his arm, 'Dukie, look!' He turns, too. 'What?' 'Over there!' 'I don't see noth—' His mouth dropped like this, Dawn, I swear it. He grabbed on to me and me to him. We was shaking like leaves in a windstorm."

"What did you see?"

She pauses, letting the moment stretch out. "I seen a body, only it wasn't solid—it was milky-like. You could see its heart pulsing in its chest. Its eyes was holes, with blood around them."

"Duke saw it, too?"

"He saw it, and it scared the bejesus out of him, just like it did me. Only he didn't want to admit that, so later he claimed he didn't see nothing."

"Maybe it was a dream."

She looks hard at me. "That's what my folks said. But it wasn't no dream, Dawn, because I heard it."

"What did it say?"

"It said . . ." She stops for a minute, to remember. "Said—moaning-like—'Dawn, I waaaaaant.'"

"Want what?"

"It didn't tell that part, or else the truck was past by then. So I never found out."

We're both snuggled in our beds. The light from the hall outside creeps under my door like oozy fingers. I show Charlotte. "Ooooooooh," she says. Just the way she says it makes me scared.

"You gonna fall asleep now, Dawn?"

"I'm going to try."

"Me too." She yawns, as if the story and the oozy fingers don't even frighten her. "Good night."

31

We wake up laughing, 'cause Little Chief is on my bed. He's not allowed in the house, so we don't know how he got here. He's looking all around, then he walks over my face as if it's part of the scenery. Charlotte starts calling him, whispering, "Here, kitty, kitty . . ." He jumps onto the windowsill, leaps back onto the bed. I hear Aunt Van in the hallway, so I stuff him under the covers. She knocks, then opens the door: "Good morning, girls."

"Good morning."

"How about some pancakes?"

"Yes, please," Charlotte says sweetly. Little Chief's wriggling under the sheet behind my leg. I put my hand down to hold him still.

"What time did you get to sleep?"

"Not too late." Charlotte looks at me. She can tell I'm having a hard time. "We'll be down soon," she says.

"Would you like bacon or sausage?"

Little Chief scratches my hand. "Oww!"

Aunt Van gives me a puzzled look. "Bacon, please," Charlotte says quickly. She slides out of bed, grabs the blouse. "I'll get dressed now."

"I'll bet you'd like some privacy."

Charlotte nods. After the door closes, we press our hands against our mouths to shush our giggling. I throw the sheet back, and Little Chief leaps out. He glares at me, steps onto the windowsill. I open the window and watch as he climbs backward down the gutter spout.

"Close one," Charlotte says.

☼

We're almost finished with breakfast when Ram comes. Elvis is playing, and Aunt Van's singing along, swinging her hips to the beat of "Treat Mc Nice." Ram knocks on the door, but it's Charlotte he's looking for, not me.

"What is it?"

He waits til she's outside.

"Jimbo said your mom wants you."

We can tell by his face that something's wrong.

"Where is she?" Charlotte asks.

"In the barn—he said you'd know where."

She takes off running, and I follow, with Ram right behind.

Charlotte doesn't even look back. She races down the driveway, over the field, to the gravel road that runs past her house. She's fast; I can't keep up. "Hey, wait!" I call, but she doesn't answer.

We get closer. I see that her dad's truck is gone. The front door of the house is standing open. In the back of my head Aunt Van says, "Close it, Dawn, the flies are getting in." But Charlotte runs right past. Somewhere way behind, Ram is running after me.

She goes through the sliding door into their barn. In the ten seconds it takes for me to get there, she's disappeared. I run down the wide cement corridor, flanked by rows of empty stanchions, calling her. My footsteps echo from the walls. I stop at the end, turn around, run back. Ram's just coming through the door. "Where is she? Where'd she go?" I ask.

He must have played hide-and-seek with Rufe and Sonny here, because he snakes through the old tank room, back to where a wooden door is bolted to the wall. He lifts a lever, and it slides partway open on a metal track. Suddenly Jimbo's on the other side, blocking the way. "No, Dawn," he says. His short, square jaw is set.

"What do you mean?"

"Ma said no."

But as he answers I get one leg through and slide my body after, darting sideways to slip beyond his reach. "Hey, stop," he says; but I rush on. Behind me Ram is arguing; in front there's darkness and sweltering heat. I walk face first into a wall of hay. The dust is so thick, it's like breathing bits of straw. I feel ahead of me: bales everywhere. On the other side of the hay, someone's crying. "Charlotte," I call. "Let me through."

Then Jimbo's behind me, grabbing my arm: "Dawn, I told you not to come back here."

"What happened? Who's crying?" In the darkness I can hardly see his face.

"You have to leave."

"I won't!"

He gives up then. He moves away. Suddenly, in front of him, there's a dim strip of light. The light grows into a square as he shoves a hay bale to the side, then climbs through the hole. Quick, before he can block it up again, I follow.

No one sees me. They're gathered around something: Sonny, Jimbo, Charlotte, and her mom. Sonny's crying, a flat, high wail. A kerosene lamp hangs from the rafters, but the light is dim. The heat and dust are awful. I move up, to see what they're looking at. There's something long and dark stretched out on the floor. It looks like a bundle of old cloth, rags maybe. At the far end Charlotte's mom is holding something pale. I move closer. That's when I see the face. "Hush, Dawn," she says, not even looking up. "Hush that now."

"He's dead, isn't he? He's dead!" I can't stop yelling.

"Hush, Dawn," she says again. She's washing his hair, running a cloth through it and around his neck, over and over. In between, she's speaking to him in a low, soft voice. He doesn't move or open his eyes.

"Is he dead?" I ask.

"No. If you feel right here, his heart is beating." His mom shows me a place on the side of his neck. I'm afraid to touch him. "Show her, Charlotte," Mrs. Williams says. "Show her he's alive."

But I don't want to touch him. He looks so pale and cold, even in this heat. "Should we call an ambulance?" I ask.

"I'm trying to bring him around." She doesn't stop moving her hands while she's talking.

"I'll run home and call an ambulance," I say. "They'll take him to the hospital. That's where he should be, if he's badly hurt."

She doesn't look up. "You can't do that."

"Why not?"

"We've got to handle it ourselves. We don't have the money to pay doctors. And if we went to the hospital, they might throw Bucky in jail. The doctors in Richmond put him on a special list last year."

"But they could save Rufe's life!"

"That's God's will, Dawn," she says. "Only He can decide whether Rufe will live or die."

☼

She wants us to pray. I go with the others, Charlotte and Jimbo and Sonny. They get down on their knees; Sonny's still crying, but when they start, "Our Father," he joins in through his tears. "Our Father, who art in heaven, hallowed be Thy name. . . ."

"Don't you know it, Dawn?" Charlotte asks.

"No." I'm crying, too.

"I'll teach you," she says. "Listen and say it after me."

☼

We pray and pray. In the meantime Mrs. Williams talks to Rufe, saying his name, washing his face and hair. She tells him she's sorry, that if she ever gets the money, she'll take him and the others far away, where they'll never be hurt again. She tells him that she loves him, that she never cared that he was slow in school. Rufe just lies there.

Finally, after a long time, she says for us to go.

"Charlotte and Jimmy, take Sonny in the house and give him a bath with soap. Otherwise those chicken pox are going to get infected, in all this heat and dust." They nod. She turns to me.

"Dawn, this is secret. Do you understand?"

"Yes."

"Not even that nice colored boy—what do you call him? Ram?"

I nod. I guess by doing that I'm saying yes.

✧

We're all gasping when we get outside. Right away Jimbo pulls up water from the well and wets us down. We stare at each other, not sure what to say or do. Finally Jimbo clears his throat. "Guess we best take Sonny in, like Mama said."

"What if your dad comes back?"

"He won't be home til afternoon milking's done."

"Why did he beat Rufe up?"

"'Cause he wouldn't do as he was told."

"That's wrong, beating him for that," I say; but they don't want to hear what I think. They catch hold of Sonny and take him in the house without saying good-bye.

32

I don't see them all that afternoon. I stay over at the planet, waiting for Charlotte, but she never shows. After a while Ram comes, too, only he's changed his name.

"N-n-n-not Ram," he says.

"What, then?"

"Delbert." He's sitting with his head down. Tears are splashing down his cheeks. "I'm n-n-never coming back here, ever," he says.

"You know about it?"

He nods.

"How'd you find out?"

"Jimbo told me. This morning he said, 'Go get Charlotte. Daddy hit Rufe so hard he knocked him out.' "

I nod. "They don't want anyone to know."

"Wh-wh-what if he dies?"

"They'll have to tell, I guess."

We sit for a while longer, then we each go home.

☼

The first thing I do is tell Aunt Van about the piano.

"You know those times you thought I was improving? Well that was Delbert, not me." I start crying when I tell her that.

She stares at me like she can't believe her ears. "Delbert was playing the piano?"

"Yeah, one day I let him try, and it turned out he could play better than me. So I let him practice, too."

"But I would have seen him," Aunt Van argues.

"You were always in the kitchen. And then later, when I wanted you to see, you never did." I keep on crying. She's still upset.

"All those times I complimented you, it was really him?" she asks.

I nod.

"That was dishonest, Dawn," she says.

"I know."

She walks away with her shoulders slumped, like I've disappointed her for good.

☼

I walk back to Charlotte's. The door's closed now. I wait outside to see if anyone will come. For a long time there's no one, then Sonny appears on the side of the porch, carrying Charlotte's messed-up doll, Marie. I call to him, "Is Rufe okay?" He doesn't even turn his head. "Sonny," I call again. "Answer." This time he looks up.

"I got the chicken pox," he says slowly. "I'm real, real sick. You shouldn't talk to me, or you might get it, too."

"I already had it, Sonny. That's why I played Chutes and Ladders that day, remember?"

"Yeah." Sonny seems dazed. "And you wanted to see them pictures, didn't you, Dawn?"

"That's not important, now, Sonny. What's important is, is Rufe better? Did he come to?"

"Mama's taking real good care of him."

"Where's Charlotte?"

"She don't want to see no one right now. She said if I'll play by myself, I can have Marie to keep me company."

"That's good."

"I'd rather have a real person—like you. Could we go to the planet, so I can see the bugs?"

"Maybe later, Sonny. First I want to talk to Charlotte."

She doesn't want to open her door. I stand there and wait. "You got to let me in," I say.

"Go away, Dawn. This don't concern you."

"It does, too."

"Tomorrow you're going back. Then you can pretend none of it happened."

"I can't pretend, either. I saw him down there, Charlotte. I want to know if he's all right."

"He's all right," she says. Her voice is flat.

"Charlotte, could I open the door just a crack?"

I stand there a couple more minutes, but she never says yes.

33

Next day, they claim he fell and banged his head. "He knocked himself out down in the barn," Jimbo says, as if he hasn't seen me for a while. "If we hadn't found him, he could have died."

"Why are you telling lies like that?" I ask. "You know what really happened. And it could happen to you."

"If Daddy goes to jail, where would we live? Did you ever think about that, Dawn? We wouldn't even have a house, because this house comes with his work."

I just stand there, staring at Jimbo, and he stares back. He's always been short and kind of fat, but he seems taller now. Charlotte won't speak to me at all. When she sees me coming, she turns her back and runs away.

Sonny and I go to Planet Kid. Del's here, too. In an hour or so, he'll be gone for good, 'cause his parents came. Sonny's got Charlotte's doll, Marie. He used a crayon to make red dots all over her face.

"She's got the chicken pox, like me. Only she's a baby, so she cries about it. I'm big now. I'm never going to cry about the chicken pox again."

"That's 'cause they don't hurt you anymore. See, they're starting to heal."

We both look at his arms and legs. The blistery red spots are turning pink.

"How's Rufe?" I ask. Sonny looks confused, like he knows he's not supposed to say certain things, but he can't remember what they are.

"Rufe's hurt," he says sadly. "He can't play with me no more."

"Can Del and me go see him? We won't say anything about . . . you know."

"Maybe." He's playing in the dirt, then he looks up. "You can see him through the window, Dawn. He's lying on the front-room couch."

Del looks at me. I think we're feeling the same thing: like we're scared to go down there, because we know the truth. But I want to see Rufe before I leave. If I don't go now, I might not get another chance.

"Are you coming?" I ask Del.

"N-n-n-n-no."

"You won't know what happened, if you don't."

"Could you call me on the phone and let me kn-kn-kn-know?"

"No," I said, "I won't."

He stands up then and squares his shoulders, like he did when he was the general; and I see that he is going to come, after all.

☀

Sonny leads us down. We don't go right across the yard; instead we dodge and crouch between cars, as if there's danger all around. The window of the front room's partway open. We crawl there on our hands and knees. Then I raise myself up and peek over the sill.

Rufe's stretched out on his back on the faded couch. His eyes are closed when I look in, and he's alone. Though the room is shadowed, I can see the bruises: one almost covers the left side of his face; the other's under his right eye. He stirs, picks up a glass of water from the table by the couch, and drinks. Then, suddenly, he opens his eyes and looks at me. I think maybe he's just waking, so I smile and wait, but his face is blank. Del pulls on my shorts; "Dawn, I think I hear someone."

"Hey, Rufe," I whisper. "Rufe, it's me."

He turns his head as if he can't tell where the sound is coming from.

"Here," I whisper, "in the window. I want to say good-bye."

He moans then, but when he turns his head again, he sees me. I can't tell what he thinks. I take Del by the shoulders and move him in the window, too. He's trembling, but he raises his hand and waves at Rufe before we run away.

☼

Charlotte doesn't come to say good-bye, not to Del or me, either; but she sends a crumpled note: *See you next time you come down.* Auntie Merle stays in her doorway, so I'm the only one standing in the yard waving when his family's car pulls out.

His mom and dad were nice. They seemed glad that Del had made a friend. Carrie teased him: "Don't tell me you stayed Delbert for the whole summer. I thought sure you'd have them calling you something else by now."

We didn't tell her much. One time she looked at all the grass and trees and asked, "What did you do out here in the sticks all summer, anyway?"

"We hung around."

Our eyes met. "Del's good on the piano," I told his sister. "He can play most any song, if he sees somebody play it once."

She looked surprised. "You'll have to play for me, squirt."

He frowned, but I saw that he was pleased.

☼

Before he left he took me to one side. "You're going to call me, right, Dawn?"

I had his number on a little piece of paper. "I'll call you, Del. I'll call you Monday night."

He nodded. I was pretty sure what he was feeling. We were the only ones—besides Charlotte's family—who knew what really happened to Rufe.

34

It's so great to see my mom. She doesn't even wait until the car is parked; when it's opposite the porch she flings the side door open and gets out. She has a metal crutch, with a handle up above her elbow, to lean on, but she comes across the grass in long strides, the way she used to walk, and wraps me in her arms. She smells like turpentine and perfume mixed. I tell her that. She laughs out loud. "I made Doug take me to the studio last night, just for a minute. After you guys, there's nothing I've missed as much as painting." She cups her hands around my face. "You look older, Dawn. And you're so brown. You must have spent the whole summer outdoors."

Aunt Van and Uncle Moody line up for hugs, so I go back and kiss my dad and pick up Beth first, then Timmy. They've grown, too. Beth can talk in sentences: "Dawn, where's pony?" she asks, then pulls my hand: "Let's see." Timmy's got his little violin. I tell him about Del. "Maybe when we're back in Washington, he'll come over, and the two of you can play duets." His face lights up.

Seeing them, I almost forget about the Williams. We're busy: first we bring Star up from the barn. She snorts and rests her head against Mom's chest. Beth dances around her, feeding her bits of grass. Uncle Moody and Dad are talking baseball. I get my glove; Dad whistles when he sees how hard I throw, and how my curve breaks to the left. We have a picnic on the porch: chicken and dumplings, sliced tomatoes, biscuits, corn on the cob, and chocolate cake. I watch Mom eat. Her fingers are a little bent, from the arthritis, but she's never had it badly in her hands and arms. She's laughing, wiping the cake crumbs from her mouth, pointing to something out beyond the hills. Everybody else is laughing, too, not at the joke but just because we see that she's so happy and alive. It feels like she's come back from another land, a place that's cold and far away.

After supper I take Timmy to Planet Kid. He's nervous, like he always is in the country, wondering if something's going to jump out from behind the weeds and bite him. But once we get there, and I pull out the pillows, he seems to relax. "It's like a secret fort, isn't it? We could hide here, and no one would ever find us." "It's just for kids," I tell him then. "The grown-ups don't know about it. So don't tell, okay?"

He looks surprised when I ask him that, as if maybe he's older than he thought. "Okay."

We lie around a while. He tells me what it was like in Connecticut, staying with Aunt Margie. "The twins would wake up every night begging for ice cream. Then Beth would wake up, too. Then I would, too, and Aunt Margie would pile us all in the car in our pajamas. We'd go to the all-night Howard Johnson's and get cones." I tell him about the times we tricked the boys, and Delbert's names, and the day that Sonny caught the mudcat, and Timmy laughs and laughs.

We're leaving when something catches my eye. Under one of the feedsacks lies an edge of color that's not usually there. I lift the bag. "Look," Timmy says. "It's someone's doll."

"Her name's Marie." I pick her up. The red spots on her face look even stranger when I hold her near me. But someone's made a bed of leaves under the burlap, and shaped a little mound of milkweed seeds into a pillow.

"Why'd they leave her here?" Timmy asks. "She'll get ruined, if she stays outdoors."

"Maybe they figured she'd be safe at Planet Kid."

Timmy's not so sure. "If it rains, she'll get wet."

"Here—I've got this. . . ." I set her down, tear a piece of plastic from the trash bag that we keep over the shelves when we're not here. I lay it underneath the burlap cover. "That ought to do the trick."

We put her back in bed. "Sleep tight," Timmy tells her. He asks, "Do you think she'll wake up in the night, like Beth?"

"Maybe. But if she does, she'll see the stars. She'll make a wish, and then fall back to sleep again."

"Like us, right, Dawn?"

"Like us."

❖

We leave early the next morning. I'm still sleepy when Uncle Moody and Aunt Van fold their arms around me. The mist is rising on the county road; Dad's holding a steaming cup of coffee while he drives. The little kids fall asleep in the backseat, then I do, too. When I wake up we're somewhere outside Fredericksburg. We talk about school starting next week. Mom has a commission to do murals for the National Park Service. One of Dad's galleries is opening a new show at the end of September. Monday he'll try to find a violin teacher for Timmy.

Then the buildings of Washington come into view. We leave the highway and move onto the downtown streets. It's Sunday, so they're quiet. There's no ball game at the stadium, because the Senators are playing in Boston. We park in the lot at the apartment. "I'll make pancakes for supper," Mom says as we squeeze into the elevator. "I'll make thousands, 'cause that's how happy I am." I don't know how many she really makes, but it's platefuls and platefuls. We eat them with jam and syrup and honey and apple butter until there isn't a single one left.

I get ready for sleep in my own bed, in my own room. My baseball posters are on the walls, the way I left them, and my teddy bears Max and Andy keep guard over my pillow. I stuff my clothes into the bureau, put my cards away, dust off my special ball. Mom and Dad kiss me good-night. Afterward they're laughing and talking in the hall. I hear Mom say she may go to her studio for a while. I lie down, pull the covers up, and close my eyes. That's when it happens.

They come like a parade: Sonny in his filthy tee shirt; Jimbo, chest puffed out, like he's in charge; Rufe, with his warm lips and meadow smell; Charlotte laughing, kissing Star, playing with Little Chief, hugging me, telling stories. With them comes heat, and darkness, and the smell of straw.

I don't want them here. I try to argue them away: *This is my room, where I should be happy. Now that Mom's better, I don't have to worry about anything.* To protect myself, I put them on the far side of a wall of facts: the Senators' batting order, the players' averages, the pitchers' ERAs. I list Camilo Pascual's victories: eight shut-outs, a one-hitter, a two-hitter, four five-hitters, a record so good that even Casey Stengel says he's the best pitcher in baseball. I review the Senators' schedule: Boston, Detroit, then New York. When they get back to Washington, Dad says we'll go and see them play. Thinking just of that, I hug my brown bear, Andy, til I fall asleep.

But later in the night they come again. The church-bell rings on Harvard Avenue; then someone calls me in a far-off voice. I know I'm dreaming, but I sit up in the dark, look to the window. A pale shape floats behind the glass. It has holes that look like they were torn in an old rag. Words come creeping through the glass like wind: "I waaaant . . ."

I shove the covers in my mouth to keep from yelling, turn away quickly. When I look again, it's gone. My heart is pounding. I wake up enough to call out. Dad comes, bringing me a glass of milk.

"Bad dream?"

I nod, but I don't tell him what it was. He rubs my back until I fall asleep.

The second dream is good. This time I'm sitting in a car on the highway, headed I don't know where. Beth and Timmy are asleep beside me. Mom and Dad are sleeping in the front seat; their faces are peaceful, smiling. Dad's hands are lying in his lap, but I don't mind, because the car is steering itself. The other cars are, too. They're moving slow and easy, light as giant cardboard cut-outs. Then the old Buick pulls up alongside.

At first they don't see me. Rufe's freckled hands are resting on the plastic steering wheel; and Charlotte's beside him, chattering away, pointing at this and that outside the window. Sonny's on Jimbo's lap in the back-seat. He's wearing blue flannel pajamas with cowboys on them. He's the one who turns and sees it's me.

"Hey, Dawn!" He sticks his arm out the window, then his head. "Dawn, we're here!"

They all see me then. They start waving and yelling, and I wave back. Rufe's smiling that easy smile. Charlotte's squealing, "Dawn!"

I'm happy, but confused. "Are we in Virginia?"

"Not anymore!"

"Where are we, then? Where are we going?"

"We're heading out," Rufe says. "We're going to a place that's safe for kids."

"Like Disneyland?"

"No—better than that, because it's free."

"Where is it, then?"

He shrugs, like he's not sure, but they're all smiling. Jimbo's got that hatchet on the seat beside him, like a pet. They wave for me to follow them.

35

Someone whispers in my ear: *"If I had the money, I'd take you far away. . . ."* I wake up, sit up in my bed, and look around. It's daylight, but there's hardly any traffic on the street, no one on the sidewalks either. I know now what I have to do.

Mr. Hooper, who lives above his shop, opens it just for me. But he argues, so I have to draw myself up tall. "I asked Mom about my baseball stuff. She said I can do whatever I like, because it's mine." He peers at me, his bushy white eyebrows brushing the tops of his wire-rimmed glasses. "What happened to you, Dawn? You've changed."

Charlotte said, *"Don't tell."* And so I lie: "I'm just not interested in baseball anymore."

He sets the ball and cards aside, and counts the bills onto the table: ten, twenty, thirty, forty, fifty, sixty, seventy. "That's top dollar," he says then.

"Thank you very much." But when my hands pick up the money, he can see they're shaking.

"Dawn," he asks, "is everything all right?"

"Yes."

I have to stop myself from fleeing out the door.

☼

Outside there's traffic now. I pass an old man on the sidewalk; he speaks, but I turn my eyes away. Pigeons scrabble in the gutter. A bus goes by, spewing exhaust; it stops and lets a woman out. She's dressed in black, as if she's on her way to church. Someone's coming round the corner, singing a song I've heard before. The voice stops in mid-verse. I look up, into Mom's face.

Her old blue jacket's splashed with paint, and she smells like turpentine. I realize her studio's just down the block. "I spent the whole night painting!" she explains happily. Then she looks at me again. "What's wrong?" she asks.

I'm so shocked to see her, I can't think. I open my mouth, but instead of words, sobs burst out. When I try to push them back, they come even stronger, like someone breaking through that walled-in hideout in the Williamses' barn, pushing the hay bales far apart and opening the room to light and air.

"What is it, Dawn?" Mom asks. Her arms are wrapped around me now.

I shake my head. Her voice is low and strong.

"Remember how you helped me when I was sick?"

I remember: changing Beth's diaper, feeding her, walking Timmy to Mrs. Glover's apartment after kindergarten.

"Let me help you now," Mom says.

-☼-

It's the first time we've been together—just her and me—for over a year. We sit across from each other in a booth at the Hot Shoppe on Sixteenth Street. She props the metal crutch against the wall. I notice lines around her mouth, and her eyes look deeper and less carefree than they used to. She reaches over and takes my hand.

"I was in my own world last year," she says. "Even before I went to the hospital, I lost touch, 'cause I was so depressed and sick. I'm sorry, Dawn."

"That's okay." I'm still wiping away tears.

"It's not okay, but I'm back now. Tell me what's going on."

I don't know where to start. It feels, suddenly, like we're strangers. I close my eyes for a minute. That's when the smells come back to me. I ask, "Did you ever spend the night down in the barn?"

"Yes. I loved listening to the animals breathe, and the way it smelled was like heaven." She smiles at me.

"That's where it begins. . . ."

I don't tell everything, 'cause some of it feels private; but I tell a lot. There are parts that make Mom laugh: Charlotte trying to scare Del out of the corncrib, and scaring me instead; our spying on Auntie Merle, and seeing her new TV. She hears about the spot under Mrs. Williams' eye, how I told Aunt Van, Duke's note, and the fight when it was found. I tell about the morning I saw Rufe down in the barn.

"His father had hurt him?" Mom's voice is even, quiet.

I nod. "He hit him in the face and knocked him out."

Mom sits still for a moment, as if she's soaking it all in. Then she shakes her head. "Dawn, I'm sorry you had to go through that."

I feel a flash of anger. "It's not about *me*, it's them!"

Mom takes a drink of coffee, stirs what's left as if the motion helps her think. "How can we help them?" she asks then. I show her the bills I got from Mr. Hooper, explain what Mrs. Williams promised in the barn. "If she had the money, she'd take them far away."

"I think she would have done that by now, if she were going to," Mom sighs.

"She didn't have the money!"

"She has family that she could have asked."

"Maybe they didn't have anything to give her."

"That's possible, but I think they would have protected those children no matter what." Mom's voice is sad. "I'm not saying we shouldn't try to help, Dawn; I'm just telling you it may not work."

"Why not?"

"Because it's hard to leave your life. No matter how good or bad it is, you get used to it. Not only that, but she has pride. She may not accept money from someone else."

"We have to try." I'm fighting to hold it back, but a tear rolls down my cheek.

She reaches over, brushes it away. "We will."

❖

She talks to Dad on the telephone. I guess he must agree, 'cause later he comes home from the bank with a hundred dollars. "I think I remember that the Parkers had cousins in North Carolina," Mom says. "Maybe Shirley could take the children there. With this and the money you got from Mr. Hooper, there's enough for bus tickets and meals along the way." She folds the bills into a piece of paper, puts it inside an envelope, sticks the small envelope inside a bigger one. I ask her, "Do you think she will?"

"I'd like to say yes, but I doubt it." Mom writes the address, sticks on a stamp. She sits still for a minute, her hands resting on the letter. Then she looks at me. "You know, Dawn, nothing's really predictable. Some things work out better than we think. Last year I'd have guessed I'd be in a wheelchair for the rest of my life." Slowly, carefully, she gets to her feet.

"We can't really know what will happen to any of us." She puts out her arm, and I go and stand beside her. "Look how tall you are," she says suddenly. Her eyes fill up with tears.

※

I'm taking the letter to the postbox on the corner. I think of Del before I get there: how I'll call tonight, and tell him that I told, and what we've done. A bus roars by, some kids shout out the window. "Hey, girl! Where you going?" Up ahead, in front of Read's Drugstore, between a street sign and a tree, the mailbox waits.

I stand beside it, holding the envelope. I imagine it resting there, inside the metal box, for the rest of the day, then stuffed into a sack inside the mailman's truck. It will go to Central to be sorted, then put into another truck, headed south. Somewhere near Lynville—or, as Charlotte would say, Podunk Central—they'll toss it in the pile for Rural Route One. The mailman's car has a sign on it: Frequent Stops. One of those will be at Uncle Moody's mailbox. I picture Uncle Moody in his faded overalls stopping the truck on his way home from the feedstore, opening the mailbox door, gathering the envelopes. His brow will furrow when he opens the one from us and finds another one inside. Most likely, he'll head down the hill right then, over to Charlotte's. I'm just praying Rufe is better, that he's sitting on the beat-up couch on their front porch, with Sonny and Jimbo and Charlotte all nearby. "Where's your ma?" Uncle Moody will say.

"In the kitchen, making supper." One of them might ask, "What's that?"

"Don't know."

He'll poke his head inside, hand the envelope to Charlotte's mom. Maybe she'll hesitate for a minute before she rips it open; maybe she'll go someplace private, and she'll see the money, and she'll draw in her breath and think, quick, where to hide it while she makes her plans.

I don't know that's going to happen, but I'm hoping. I open the mailbox lid, hold it steady, drop the letter in.